"I know I can help you, Zara!"

Tor bent his head down to kiss her. "I don't believe that a woman's body can ever forget the sensations of being made love to, whatever tricks her brain might play."

Frantically Zara tried to escape his grasp. "What makes you think I should react to you? You're not my husband. You've never made love to me."

"No? But perhaps I'd like to."

"Well, I wouldn't like it and I won't let you!"

"What harm could there possibly be in a few kisses? What are you afraid of? What is it that you don't want to remember?" Tor persisted.

But Zara did want to remember and she was afraid—afraid of her feelings for a man who was not her husband.

ANNABEL MURRAY has pursued many hobbies. She helped found an arts group in Liverpool, England, where she lives with her husband and two daughters. She loves drama: she appeared in many stage productions and went on to write an award-winning historical play. She uses all her experiences—holidays being no exception—to flesh out her characters' backgrounds and create believable settings for her romance novels.

Books by Annabel Murray

HARLEQUIN ROMANCE
2549—ROOTS OF HEAVEN
2558—KEEGAN'S KINGDOM
2596—THE CHRYSANTHEMUM AND THE SWORD
2612—VILLA OF VENGEANCE
2625—DEAR GREEN ISLE
2717—THE COTSWOLD LION
2782—THE PLUMED SERPENT

These books may be available at your local bookseller.

Don't miss any of our special offers. Write to us at the following address for information on our newest releases.

Harlequin Reader Service
901 Fuhrmann Blvd., P.O. Box 1397, Buffalo, NY 14240
Canadian address: P.O. Box 603,
Fort Erie, Ont. L2A 9Z9

ANNABEL MURRAY

land of thunder

Harlequin Books

TORONTO • NEW YORK • LONDON
AMSTERDAM • PARIS • SYDNEY • HAMBURG
STOCKHOLM • ATHENS • TOKYO • MILAN

'Dartmoor used to be called the "Land of Thunder," a name given by the people of border villages, who looked up to the growling clouds and watched the weather grow.'

Vian Smith: *Portrait of Dartmoor*

Harlequin Presents first edition November 1986
ISBN 0-373-10933-4

Original hardcover edition published in 1986
by Mills & Boon Limited

CHAPTER ONE

WHEN she regained consciousness, they told her that her name was Zara Dane, that she was twenty-three and a married woman. She had no choice but to believe them, since her brain refused to confirm or deny the information. In fact, at first, fogged by panic, it had performed no other function than that of seeing, hearing and speaking, as, tearfully, she questioned the doctor, the nurses.

'What hospital is this? What happened to me?' But, worst of all, *'Who am I?'*

Once they had reassured her that her condition was, almost certainly, only a temporary one, she found that, apart from memories concerning her past and whatever intentions she might have had for the future, she could still think and reason. Despite the shifting nightmares that accompanied her condition, she could still make analytical judgments of her situation, even though this did nothing to quell her fear, that she might *never* remember.

She'd been alone in the car, they said, when she'd been involved in the accident, from which she'd escaped with no physical damage other than a few bruises, and they handed her a mirror.

Critically, as she would have assessed a stranger, she studied her own face. This was the woman they called Zara Dane. She liked the name. Was it because they'd repeated it so often that she'd come to accept it as hers, or because it *was* her name? But then why should the doctor, the nurses, lie to her?

She was pretty. This wasn't vanity, for she still felt as though she considered a stranger's reflection. Her face was that rarity, a perfect oval, framed by a cloud of softly waving, blue-black hair. Dark, slightly irregular brows, arched in a slightly surprised line above misty, blue-grey eyes, fringed by dark, thick lashes. There was nothing outstanding, no one memorable feature, the nose small and regular, the mouth with its full complement of white, even teeth, in perfect proportion to the rest. The overall effect was of someone quiet and gentle, with only the slightest hint of stubbornness in the rounded chin, of someone who looked vaguely unhappy. It was there in the slight droop of soft, pliant lips, in the faint lines that had no business marring the forehead of one so young.

She pushed the mirror aside. There was no profit in speculation. She must accept this unknown self, as, for the time being, she must accept the other things they'd told her, the fact that she was married, that her husband would be here soon to collect her. A husband! She drew in a quick, nervous breath and lifted her hands, white, slender, with long artistic fingers. Yes, she was *almost* sure she was artistic. Had she studied art, practised it? Her thoughts came disjointedly, yet she knew this inner searching for herself was necessary.

On the third finger of her left hand was a wedding-ring. She studied its shiny surface, noting the absence of any scratches, signs of wear. It was very new looking, and it didn't look particularly expensive. Zara had an instinctive feeling that her tastes ran towards better jewellery. If only she could remember something, anything. Her lips trembled and she set them determinedly. To give way to hysteria would solve nothing and might cause a setback in her recovery. She looked up as a nurse rustled in.

'Your husband and your friend are on their way up, Mrs Dane. Perhaps when you see them your memory will return.'

Zara scarcely listened to the bright chatter. Apprehension mingled with anticipation. Would the sight of the man she must love miraculously restore her memory? Suppose it didn't? How dreadful for him too and she couldn't *pretend* to remember, that wouldn't help either of them.

Moments later, the hot, sour taste of panic in her mouth, she stared blankly at a man who might as well be a stranger. There was no feeling of familiarity to break through the fog that seemed to enshroud her and, more disastrously, no leap of the senses. She would have expected at least to feel some physical attraction towards her own husband. After all, she reasoned painfully ... it was difficult sometimes to string coherent thoughts together ... after all, memory or not, he was still the same man, she the same woman.

With a sinking heart, she realised she wasn't even drawn to his appearance. The instinct that amnesia seemed not to have destroyed told her this wasn't the type of man, that, ordinarily, appealed to her. How on earth did she come to be married to him? Would he kiss her? Would her senses recognise his touch, even if her eyes couldn't recall his features. Her fear-widened eyes registered that he was what some people would call handsome, his square face deeply tanned beneath a thatch of very closely cropped fair hair. But his pale blue eyes had a hard, wary expression and his mouth ... with a feeling of sickness, she realised he *was* about to kiss her ... his mouth repelled her, sensual rather than sensuous.

'Zara, darling,' he seemed to hesitate over the endearment. 'Thank goodness you're all right ... physically.' He had the slightest trace of an accent that her confused brain could not place. Surreptitiously, she passed tremulous fingers across her mouth in an attempt to erase the touch of his. 'Sybil and I have been distraught.'

Sybil? For the first time Zara looked at the woman who accompanied him. This was her friend? Try as she might, Zara couldn't imagine herself making a close friend of this hard-faced, red-haired woman, her thin-lipped smile surely a forced one, as though the lack of feeling were mutual. The woman bent to brush her cheek against Zara's and Zara's instincts were confirmed. This Sybil had no affection for her.

Panic increased, rising like an obstruction in Zara's throat. The doctor had said she might leave today and she was to be released into the care of these two strangers.

'Physically there's nothing wrong,' the doctor had told her, 'nothing to keep you in hospital, no injuries to the head. I'd say you've had some unpleasant experience, which, through your accident, your mind has taken the opportunity to reject.'

'But will I ever remember, if my subconscious *wants* me to forget?'

'I think you'll find it just a matter of time, Mrs Dane. My advice would be to give yourself a little while to recover from your accident.'

'Maurice, hadn't you better leave, while I help Zara dress?' Sybil's harsh voice broke in on Zara's thoughts.

She'd noticed the shabby-looking suitcase, but hadn't connected it with herself. Of course her husband would bring her clothes. Doubtfully she studied him. She was glad Sybil had saved her the embarrassment of having to ask his name. Maurice Dane? It meant nothing. He turned to leave. Strange, Zara mused, why shouldn't a husband watch his wife dress? Though she was glad he hadn't. Had she not been accustomed to change in his presence? She didn't think she'd mind if she loved a man, but she couldn't be sure.

Silently, the woman, Zara couldn't think of her as her friend, handed over undergarments, new, with no sign of wear and as she continued to dress, it dawned upon Zara that everything handed to her was unworn. She'd hoped that the sight of her possessions, her clothes, might hold some clue for her, but it wasn't so. Moreover she didn't like these clothes, the look of them, the feel of them against her smooth, olive skin. She could understand her possession of a full set of unworn clothes. As a relatively new bride, this must be her trousseau. What she couldn't understand was her own apparent lack of taste.

The arrival of her husband, the donning of her own clothes, ought to have restored a little of her self-assurance. Instead she was becoming more and more bewildered and conscious of increasing insecurity.

'Come on,' Sybil said abruptly. 'We've a long way to go and we have to talk first. You can't start a new job, in new surroundings, without knowing something about it.'

For a friend, Sybil didn't show much sympathy or tact, and a new job, new surroundings? Zara pressed the knuckles of her hand hard against quivering lips. So there was to be no return to a familiar house, street, town, where she might gradually gather up the threads of her past. She felt she'd rather remain in hospital until her memory *did* return.

They had coffee at a small café not far from the hospital gates.

'And you really can't remember, nothing at all?' Maurice Dane probed insistently, his pale blue eyes intent.

'Not a thing.' Her expression was apologetic, apprehensive. 'I'm afraid I can't even remember you, being married, or ... or anything,' she ended lamely, unable to repress a blush.

He darted a swift glance at the other woman and Zara thought she saw a glimmer of satisfaction in Sybil's expression. But why should a friend be pleased at her total lack of recall? Zara decided she had been mistaken.

'In that case,' Maurice said slowly, 'we'd better tell you a little about yourself. When I rang the hospital and they told me you'd completely lost your memory, I could hardly believe it.' Did he sound, not jubilant, that was impossible, but less regretful than one would expect of a man speaking of his wife's disability?

'Sybil mentioned a job,' Zara prompted.

'I think we'd better start further back, when we first arrived in England.' Arrived in England? Weren't they British subjects? 'We thought we'd given Australia a fair go, that it wasn't for us.' Australia! That was it, that faint twang to his voice, but was he saying she'd lived there too? 'Too right! That's where we met. By coincidence you'd decided to return to the old homeland, you and Syb that is, so we all travelled home together.'

'But when did you and I . . .?' Helplessly she revolved her loose-fitting ring.

Maurice leant forward, eyes probing into hers, speaking slowly, emphatically.

'We fell for each other on the trip over, got married when we landed.'

'How . . . how long ago?'

'Six weeks.'

Was it possible to forget six weeks of marriage? Since she could remember no other details of her past, she supposed it must be.

'We had to find work,' he continued, 'and you didn't want to lose sight of Syb so we decided we'd all stick together and we struck lucky.'

'We did?' Zara said faintly. It seemed strange that a newly married woman should want her girlfriend along, that her husband should allow it. But then she couldn't remember what sort of person she'd been before. . . .

'Yeah, a couple of weeks later, I spotted this advert. Fellow leading a secluded life looking for a housekeeper, odd-job man *and* a secretary. We applied and bingo!'

'Which am I?' Zara asked.

'The secretary.'

'But,' she said doubtfully, 'can I type, take shorthand?'

'No shorthand, but you can type well enough. He writes his stuff out. A lot of authors do.'

'An author?' Despite the gloom enshrouding her, Zara felt a spark of interest. 'What sort of books?'

'Search me. Does it matter? It's a job.'

'You said he leads a secluded life? Where exactly? Where are we now?'

'We're in Somerset.' Maurice hesitated, then: 'And he lives in Devon.' He seemed to watch her closely. 'On Dartmoor.'

'Goodness,' Zara said faintly, 'that's carrying seclusion a bit far.' At least she'd heard of Dartmoor, knew where it was.

Maurice seemed to relax. For the first time his heavy mouth curved into a smile.

'No accounting for tastes.' He pushed away his empty cup. 'Right, we'd better be on our way.'

'There's a lot I'd still like to know,' Zara objected, 'about myself, my name before I married, how I came to be in Australia. I don't feel as if I'm Australian.'

'You're not,' he agreed, 'none of us are.' He leant across the table and patted her hand. 'I know how you feel, darling girl, but it would take a hell of a time to recount your life story. Besides, don't forget, we've only known each other a short while. There's a lot about you I don't know myself.'

'But Sybil must . . . you said we were friends, before I met you?'

'Not of very long standing,' Sybil put in hastily, 'I mean comparatively speaking,' she added, as Maurice shot her a look that seemed to carry a warning. 'We weren't childhood friends or anything ... just a few months,' she ended lamely.

On just a few months' acquaintance, she, Zara, had refused to be parted, even following her marriage. What a strange person the real me must be, Zara thought anxiously.

'I think we should be on our way.' Maurice was looking impatiently at his watch. 'When Endacott wrote, he advised me to be there before dark. Apparently the moor's a tricky place at night. You'll just have to ask questions as they occur to you, Zara, and if we know the answers we'll put you wise. O.K?'

It was very far from O.K. but she had to comply.

How she hoped her memory would return soon, Zara brooded, as she followed them to the car. It would be terrible to have to rely on others for knowledge of herself and it wasn't only not knowing things. She just couldn't understand some of the details that had been revealed to her. If only these problems had arisen earlier, so she could have questioned the doctor, asked him if loss of memory could occasion drastic changes of personality, so alien to her seemed everything she was supposed to be, to have done.

The hospital where Zara had spent the last few days had been on the Somerset/Devon border. As the winter's afternoon waned towards sunset, they reached Moretonhampstead, on the edge of Dartmoor. On the moor proper, there was still enough light to see its tawny colouring, rolling lines broken by granite outcrops. Only a few sparse trees dotted the landscape, their silhouetted shapes bent in an easterly direction, showing the prevalence of westerly winds on the unprotected land.

Zara shivered. She wouldn't like to cross this bleak, inhospitable wasteland alone in daytime, let alone at night. Although it was only November, the winter seemed more advanced here than it had ... had where? How did she know it was November? She tried to beat back excitement. Perhaps she was beginning to remember, but she mustn't force it. She concentrated instead on the road. Visibility was bad. A steady rain fell, whipped from side to side in gusts of noisy wind and in the failing light, large, granite rocks loomed gloomy, sullen-looking, like fantastic, prehistoric beasts.

'What do you know about this Mr Endacott?' she ventured after a while, and Sybil answered her.

'Only what it said in the advert, and in his letter.'

'Yeah,' Maurice interposed, 'but we don't have that with us.' Almost as if he were reluctant for her to read it. But that was ridiculous. Why should her husband have any secrets from her?

'I can remember most of it,' Sybil volunteered, as if she had read Zara's thoughts. 'He said peace and quiet were essential to him, that he'd expect any staff he engaged to be efficient, but unobtrusive, discreet locally about his identity, that he had no wish to be lionised.'

'He must be quite well known,' Zara mused. 'Had you heard of him before, Maurice?'

'No, but then I'm not a great reader of books.'

This was something she and her husband didn't have in common. With a little thrill, she realised one more thing about herself, she was a voracious reader. The veil of amnesia must be lifting.

'Does Mr Endacott know about my accident, that I can't remember anything?'

'Yeah, I had to write to him, to explain why we'd be a week late.'

'And he doesn't mind?'

'Why should he? It won't affect your work.'

'I suppose not.' Zara was doubtful. She closed her eyes, visualising a typewriter keyboard, moved her fingers. She didn't feel she'd been particularly expert. She hoped Mr Endacott wouldn't be too demanding.

Their route took them through Princetown, though Zara wouldn't have known its name, if she hadn't enquired about the grim-looking building they passed, but she knew she'd heard of the isolated prison. About three miles further on, after a tangle of narrow roads, just adequate for their car, they saw ahead of them the lights of a single house.

'That must be Wolfstor Farm, Endacott's place,' Sybil exclaimed.

The headlights of the car showed the farmhouse as a large, four-square granite building. All but one of its windows were in darkness, but as the car drew to a halt, a porchlight came on and the figure of a man could be seen, a tall, dark silhouette against its sudden brightness. As Maurice Dane propelled Zara forward into the circle of light, the eyes of the man in the doorway narrowed, his lips parted and for one crazy second, Zara had the idea he was about to speak her name. But that was ridiculous since they'd never met before.

'I'm sorry we're a week later than planned,' Maurice's manner was deferential, 'but . . .' He shrugged expressively.

'Because of your wife's accident,' the other replied. 'I quite understand.' Once again his eyes turned towards Zara and this time there was an almost hostile expression in their brilliant, viridian-green depths. 'Come in.' He continued to look at Zara with a searching intensity and she felt herself flushing, as she preceded the others along the hallway of the grey moorland house.

Their employer led them into a room to the right of the hall, which, he explained, was his workroom.

'I'm Tor Endacott,' he said. 'Mr Dane I've written to of course. Perhaps, Dane, you'd introduce the ladies.'

'Sybil Chalmers, housekeeper . . . and my wife, Zara, your secretary.'

Zara held out her hand, to find it encompassed in long, lean fingers, which immediately exerted steely pressure on her own. Was it her imagination, or did he retain her hand a fraction of a second longer than he'd held Sybil's? His flesh was pleasant to the touch, warm and dry and . . . disconcertingly, Zara felt a distinct tingling sensation, spreading from the contact of her fingers with his, as her heart performed strange, independent actions that left her slightly breathless. Hurriedly, she snatched her hand away and saw a faint curl of his beautifully moulded mouth, as if he'd realised the reason for her abrupt action, before she lowered her eyes, in a belated attempt to hide her confusion. Tor Endacott was a most attractive man. In fact, he positively emanated virile masculinity, but she had no business to be aware of it, to react to it . . . a married woman.

Although he was talking principally to Maurice, Zara felt those strange green eyes return to her again and again, but their earlier antagonism had been replaced by a steady, controlled, expressionless survey of her, which she found disconcerting. But despite her embarrassment, Zara made her own covert study of Tor Endacott. She'd been confidently expecting their employer to be an elderly, pedantic professor and this man was a complete revelation to her . . . very tall, about six foot two or three and lean, with aristocratically chiselled features. He wasn't overly handsome, she decided, but he was certainly distinguished looking. The clean-cut lines of his face, straight nose and well-shaped mouth were complemented by hair slightly less disciplined than the rest of his appearance, being wavy and chestnut in colour and a little overdue for the barber's attentions. His voice was like the man himself, crisp, controlled, but with a faint, attractive huskiness in its depths.

'No doubt you'd like to see your rooms?' he enquired at length. 'When you've freshened up, there'll be a meal available. The last one, I hope,' he added humorously, 'that I'll be called upon to prepare. Afterwards, we can discuss your various duties, particularly those of my secretary.' Again his brilliant green glance moved in Zara's direction and again she received the impression she'd gained at her first sight of him, that there was something distinctly hostile in his gaze. What could he possibly have against her, a complete stranger?

Sybil's small room was situated above the entrance porch, between a spare room and the master bedroom, whilst that allotted to Zara and Maurice was at the rear of the house . . . twin beds, Zara was relieved to see.

'If you'll join me in the kitchen when you're ready?' With a brief nod and a final, curious glance at Zara, Tor Endacott left them to settle in.

As well as the suitcase Maurice had brought to the hospital, there was a second, larger one and as Zara unpacked their contents and hung them in the fitted wardrobe, she reflected again upon the utter lack of taste exhibited by the clothes she handled.

'Will you change?' Maurice asked her. He hadn't bothered to unpack, but was sitting on the edge of one of the beds, smoking a cigarette and watching her, a curiously intent expression on his face. What was he thinking? Zara hoped that, now they were alone together, he wasn't going to . . . to . . .

'I . . . I don't think so.' She was reluctant to undress in front of him . . . in front of her own husband? She sought for a plausible excuse, which wouldn't give offence. 'It's hardly worth it, is it? I mean . . . for a couple of hours?'

In the long mirror of the wardrobe, she was, for the first time, able to assess herself in full and as she brushed out the luxuriant waves of her smoky-dark hair, she could detect glaring faults in the dress she'd worn for her journey. It appeared to be a size too large and was a hideous shade of pink, which she felt sure she would never have chosen. The whole effect was of an outfit, hastily, carelessly selected. Even in the most pressing circumstances, surely it would have been possible to find clothes more suited to her slight, petite stature ... five foot three, she guessed, certainly no more than a size twelve, her legs slender with trim ankles and dainty feet. Only her breasts were generous, burgeoning full and high above her tiny waist.

About to retouch her mouth with a lipstick, taken from a cheap, plastic handbag, she recoiled from the shocking pink that matched the dress and decided to do without. She hoped fervently there would be an opportunity for shopping, so she could supply the deficiencies of both wardrobe and cosmetics.

The kitchen wasn't difficult to locate. They had merely to follow the appetising smell. It was a large, cheerful room, furnished in pine, teamed with modern fitmets and heated by a navy Aga stove. Blue willow-pattern pottery gleamed on the enormous dresser and on the table, set ready for their meal.

Maurice and Sybil did ample justice to the delicious hotpot, but Zara could only toy with the food. She was decidedly apprehensive about the future, particularly about working for Tor Endacott, convinced he would prove to be an exacting employer. She also had this feeling every time she accidentally met his eyes, that something about her was annoying him.

The meal over, Tor invited them to bring their coffee into the sitting-room, next to the kitchen. It was a warm, inviting apartment, where clever use had been made of existing pine cupboards, the colour-scheme of the furnishings in pinks and browns. Despite her apprehension, Zara found herself relaxing on the soft comfort of a deep, old-fashioned sofa, making herself known to its prior, sole occupant, a large, ginger cat, which graciously accepted her advances. She felt quite envious of Sybil, who would have the running of the house. Its interior was homelike, making her almost able to forget the wild, bleak setting outside, her personal, inner loneliness.

When it came to discussing Zara's tasks, to her dismay, Tor suggested that Sybil and Maurice retire, since the details would scarcely be of interest to them and might take some considerable time. They didn't appear too happy about this considerate suggestion, but could scarcely dispute it. Zara didn't relish being left alone so soon with her new employer. But he was aware of her amnesia so he was unlikely to probe for information she couldn't supply. She wondered if Maurice had submitted references on her behalf and wished she could see them. The names of her referees, her past appointments might hold vital clues to earlier times. She was surprised in any case that a man should employ three newcomers to his country. Australia was rather distant for the satisfactory taking up of references.

As the door closed behind her husband and Sybil, she felt herself go tense. Without their supportive knowledge of her, she felt vulnerable and alone. Moreover, there was something about this man which disturbed her, though what it was she couldn't have said, attributing it to her unusually sensitive and nervous frame of mind since her accident, the sense she still had that he was hostile to her.

She clasped and unclasped her slender hands, trying to look intelligent and efficient. She wished he would sit down, instead of leaning against the fireplace, hands thrust deeply into trouser pockets, studying her in that critical, almost disapproving fashion, his stance emphasising lean hips and strong thighs. She wished he would say what had to be said and then let her escape.

When he did speak, it was not of his work, and what he said was so unbelievable and, in the circumstances, so cruel, that she could only stare up at him, her soft, pliant lips trembling with shock.

'And now, *Mrs Dane,*' his voice was hard, cynical, insinuative, 'now that we're alone, perhaps you'll tell me, *have you really lost your memory?*'

CHAPTER TWO

HIS words struck like a blow to the solar plexus and it was some while before she could answer, swallowing first the lump of misery and resentment lodged in her throat.

'I . . . I don't understand. What do you mean? Of course I've lost my memory.'

'I see!' His expression of cynical disbelief hadn't altered one whit and she realised with increasing indignation that he really didn't credit her mental state.

'You don't believe me,' she accused, blue-grey eyes darkening with hurt, with anger. 'If you knew how . . . how horrible it is,' she choked back a sob. 'Why should I lie about such a dreadful thing? It . . . it's terrifying, waking up to find you don't know who you are, where you've come from, where you're going.'

'But then your *husband* will have filled in these gaps?' His manner was hatefully sarcastic.

'Yes, but it isn't the same as knowing, being able to remember for myself.'

'Presumably you *can* remember how to type?' he asked drily. 'Because, frankly, you're no use to me if you can't.'

'Maurice says I can, and I think I can . . . I . . .'

'Well, you can try the typewriter tomorrow,' he told her brusquely. He began to pace up and down, his unusual eyes still intent upon her pale, drawn face. 'I can't believe it,' he muttered, 'it's too utterly incredible.'

'Why is it?' she demanded with an attempt at spirit. 'Plenty of people suffer from amnesia, why not me? Why should *you* disbelieve me?'

'You seriously expect me to believe that you remember nothing at all?'

'Of course!' she snapped. 'Because it's true.' She shook her dark head despairingly. 'All I can recall,' her words came disjointedly, 'is waking up and realising ... then the awful fear ... I don't remember the accident, where I was going, why ...' It occurred to her that she hadn't asked Maurice these questions. Presumably he would have the answers to such recent events? 'All I know,' she added, her tone one of unconscious pathos, 'is what I've been told, my name, age, where I come from, why I'm here. I keep wondering if it wouldn't be best for me to go back to Australia, and. ...'

'*To Australia?*' His tone was sharp. 'But ...'

'I thought perhaps familiar surroundings, people I'd worked with ...'

'Hold on!' he interrupted, 'you're no Australian.' He sounded accusing.

'I'd realised that much!' she told him with dignity. 'None of us are. Maurice and Sybil had been out there longer, of course, long enough to pick up an accent and ...'

'That's what *they* told you?'

'Naturally!' she almost shouted. 'Since *I* don't remember ...'

'And how long have you been married?'

'Six weeks.'

His green eyes narrowed at her.

'So how do you know that?'

Zara was beginning to feel less sorry for herself and a growing anger with him. The utterly unfeeling boor, to cross-question in this fashion someone only just released from hospital, someone whose brain didn't feel equal to the struggle of arguing.

'I know because my husband told me.'

'And did you remember *him* by any chance?' Tor asked curiously, a strange expression in his eyes.

'No,' she said shortly.

'Odd, that,' he said provocatively, 'that you shouldn't remember the person closest to you, with whom you'd been on such *intimate* terms. Are you sure he's telling you the truth? Seen your marriage lines?'

Fiery colour ran up under her translucent skin. Did he have to be so personal, bringing up the subject that troubled her most? Unfeelingly, he continued to probe, studying her reactions.

'You can't recall what it feels like, to be kissed, to be . . .'

'No!' she rapped the word out this time, before he could go any further and because he was looking at her in a way that was making her feel decidedly uneasy. '*Why* are you asking me all these questions, Mr Endacott? If you think you haven't been told the truth, you'll have to ask my husband, or my friend. *They're* not suffering from amnesia.'

'I don't recall implying that you weren't telling the truth,' he said, smoothly, innocently, and Zara's eyes widened, smoky-blue, reproachful pools. He most certainly had . . . at least, it had seemed to her. 'But,' he added, 'it's my experience that most women bend the truth anyway, and if I ever find out that you're . . .' He paused, then: 'Oh, what the hell! You'd better go to bed, get some rest. Amnesia or not, you'll be working extremely hard whilst you're here. I don't take on passengers.'

She jumped up to face him, standing tall, making the most of her five foot three inches.

'If you don't find me suitable, or you aren't satisfied with my work, you can always dismiss me.'

'And lose myself a housekeeper and odd-job man into the bargain? Oh, go to bed. It's late.' Suddenly he too sounded weary.

She glared at him. It was so unfair. Not only had she to bear the fear and uncertainty of her loss of memory, but, for want of any other alternative, she was forced to work for this hateful man, who had seized the very first opportunity of their being alone to insult her, to insinuate. . . . If only she need not stay, if only she could remember on what terms she stood with her husband. Would he be prepared to leave this isolated place, the employ of this arrogant man, for her sake? It came to her painfully, that she just didn't know, didn't know her own husband, or what she could ask of him. She turned away, but not in time to hide the uprush of tears, which welled over and trickled down her pale, tired face.

'Tears now?'

The utter brute. He sounded increasingly uncaring and despite all her efforts a sob escaped her. She heard him swear, move swiftly to stand behind her. Then two iron hands on her shoulders swung her around to face him.

'I thought so! A woman's final resort.' He sounded as if he had no time for her sex. Then, and he spoke abruptly, as if it were alien to his nature to show kindness, 'Look, I'm sorry if I'm mistaken, but ... oh hell, it all seems too pat. Anyway, just accept, will you, that I had my reasons for thinking you might be play-acting?'

'What reasons? Tell me,' she begged.

'No. If you really have lost your memory you wouldn't undetstand. And now forget it, hmmn?' With an impatient gesture he handed her his own handkerchief, then turned his back on her, moving towards the fireplace, staring down into its dying embers. 'Go to bed, Zara Dane,' he commanded.

Slowly, she made her way upstairs, towards the bedroom she was to share with a husband she still couldn't remember, and this thought stayed her already dragging feet. Suppose ... would he expect her to ... to ...? Almost she turned back, to ask Tor Endacott if she could have a separate room. But what made her think she could make such an appeal to *him*? He would just laugh in her face, and, more to the point, what would Maurice think of such a request? He would have every right to be both hurt and offended and until her memory returned, she was totally dependent upon his goodwill. If only she could recapture a few details, the important ones, such as the love and reliance she must once have felt for Maurice, in order to have linked her life with his ... *the rest of her life*! Marriage in Zara's book was for ever. Timidly, she entered their room. Maurice was already in bed, smoking and glancing through a newspaper. Did he *have* to smoke in the bedroom?

'You were long enough. What kept you?'

'Oh,' she gestured vaguely, whilst she wondered whether to share her unhappiness with him. 'This and that.'

'So you know what he expects of you? Think you can cope?' He sounded anxious.

'I . . . I don't know. We didn't talk much about work.'

'What then?' The pale blue eyes had taken on an expression of suspicion. Was Maurice Dane a jealous husband?

'Mr Endacott was asking me about my loss of memory.' Her voice rose in remembered indignation. 'He practically accused me of . . . of *faking* it!'

Maurice dropped the newspaper and sat up straighter.

'But you're not!' He rapped out the words.

Her eyes widened. Oh no, not him too! What was the matter with everyone? Her voice trembled as she answered.

'Maurice, you of all people must know I'm not, when . . . when I can't even remember you.'

'Yes . . . yes,' he relaxed, 'of course I know you're not pretending. I didn't mean to sound as if . . . I was just agreeing that you're not putting it on. That's why . . .' he paused and she thought he looked vaguely embarrassed, 'that's why I thought you might prefer this set up.' He gestured to the separate beds.

'Oh, Maurice,' she said gratefully, 'that *was* thoughtful of you. I do hope I get my memory

back soon . . . for your sake too.' She wondered
awkwardly if she should go over and kiss him,
but somehow she couldn't bring herself to do so.

Instead, she asked him a question, with a
would-be casualness that disguised the fearful
thumping of her heart. He might be angry,
thinking she was doubting his word, but
something Tor Endacott had said had made her
realise just how little proof Maurice had
produced of his words.

'I don't suppose you happen to have our . . .
marriage lines with you? I . . .'

'Why?' he returned sharply and then, with an
obvious effort at moderating his tone, 'As it
happens, I have. Want to see then, do you? Want
concrete proof?'

'Oh no . . . no . . . I mean . . . I *would* like to see
then . . . not because I . . . I don't believe you or . . .
or anything. I . . . I thought it might help me
remember.'

'Fair enough!' He shrugged, slid out of bed and
went to the wardrobe, retrieved his wallet from
an inside pocket of his jacket. 'Here!' He passed
her a folded piece of paper.

Her fingers trembling slightly, Zara spread it
out. The licence was written out in a scholarly,
old-fashioned hand, but in one or two places the
ink had run, making a word here and there
indecipherable. One of these was Maurice's
name, of which only the letter 'M' was
identifiable, but when she commented on this, he
had an explanation.

'Yes . . . sorry about that. We'll have to send
off for another copy. It was my silly fault. I was
so chuffed with it . . . being a married man and so

on . . . I took it out to show some of our guests. There was a sudden shower, hence the smudges. As it is, I don't suppose it helps.'

'No,' she admitted, though she had gleaned two pieces of information; her maiden name 'Sinclair' and the fact that she was a commercial artist. Against Maurice's name was the one word 'Unemployed'. Still it *was* proof . . . of a kind.

'Oh well,' Maurice muttered, 'no use trying to push your memory. Just let things take their course.'

Did he mean their marriage or . . .? Either way, she felt grateful for his forbearance. He showed even more understanding by ostentatiously turning his back towards her.

'I daresay you'd like to get undressed?'

Overwhelmed with relief, she did as he suggested. He must have tremendous self-control, despite all appearances to the contrary . . . that sensual mouth. He must also be a very good, considerate man, unlike their new employer. What a pity! The thought crossed her mind that, had Tor Endacott combined her husband's kindness and consideration with his own physical attractions, instead of being such a sceptical swine, he would have been much more the type of man to whom she would have expected to find herself married. Swiftly she banished the notion as verging on the disloyal. Yet, despite her efforts, her dislike of Tor, his image seemed to linger with her, fraught with a threat she couldn't define. In a further attempt to dispel foolish fancies, she raised the question of the car crash.

'Maurice, how did my accident happen?'

'I'd hoped you wouldn't ask that,' he muttered. He seemed to select his words with care. 'I didn't want you to have anything else to worry about.'

'I'd rather know,' she insisted.

'O.K. But I don't want you to think our marriage wasn't working out. It was, and it will. We'd had a bit of a tiff. Things got heated. You said you were leaving me, rushed out, took the car. I came out of the hotel just in time to see it happen ... a narrow car-park exit, a blind bend. You didn't stop to look. There was the most God-awful sound of tortured metal . . .'

'But the car *looks* all right?' she puzzled.

'It's not the same one. The other was a write-off!'

'Oh!' Zara felt guilty, even though the incident might not have happened for all that she could recall. 'Could ... could we afford a new one?'

'Not very well,' he said drily, 'which is why we have to make a go of this job.'

'We will,' she assured him. 'I'll try, I promise. Maurice, I'm sorry I can't remember any of it, but if it was my fault, I . . .'

'Forget it,' he said magnanimously. 'Reckon I was just as much to blame for the row. But I'd rather you didn't drive again just yet.'

'No ... of course I won't,' she agreed readily.

He returned his attention to the newspaper, lit another cigarette and Zara was left to her thoughts. She wondered about their argument. It must have been something serious for her to have left in such a towering rage. She had an idea she wasn't easily angered. Perhaps it was as well for their marriage that she couldn't remember the subject of their disagreement.

On the verge of sleep, she heard a slight sound and opened her eyes to see the dim shape of Maurice moving in her direction. Immediately, her mouth went dry and she felt sure her quickened heartbeats must be audible. Had he found that, after all, he couldn't share a room with her without ...? But he didn't stop, continuing on towards the door, which he opened and closed behind him so softly, that if she hadn't been awake, she wouldn't have known of his departure. Then sleep claimed her relief-slackened body and she didn't hear his return.

Next morning, when Zara woke, Maurice had already dressed and gone downstairs. Of course an odd-job man would keep earlier hours than a secretary. There were a few animals to be tended, even though Wolfstor was no longer run as a proper farm. Such animals as there were, were kept for the sake of self-sufficiency, in case of a hard winter. It was possible, Tor had told them, for the moors to be completely inaccessible for many weeks.

She breakfasted with Sybil, who told her their employer had also risen early and had been at work in his study for almost an hour, leaving instructions that Zara was to go in as soon as she had eaten.

'It's all right for some,' Sybil commented in her harshly accented voice, 'rolling out of bed, to find the house warm and food already prepared.'

'We could swap jobs,' Zara said eagerly. 'I wouldn't mind.' She wasn't looking forward to encountering Tor Endacott again, meeting those disbelieving green eyes of his.

'No go!' Sybil said succinctly. 'I can't type for toffee.'

Tor's workroom was economically furnished, uncluttered, its predominant colour-scheme a rich, warm red, which contrasted strongly with the grey November day outside. His desk stood beneath the window with a view over rolling moorland. A small built-in fixture, on which stood a typewriter, was obviously for her use. She hesitated in the doorway, feeling extremely self-conscious and not only about meeting Tor again, but about her appearance.

It had taken her a long time to decide what she should wear, not because she was spoilt for choice, but because she couldn't decide which of the items in her wardrobe was least obnoxious to her. She had settled in the end for a badly cut grey flannel skirt and an overlarge sweater in a harsh green and although the sweater was too big, the fullness of her breasts did, in some measure, compensate for its unlovely, graceless lines.

'Come in! Come in!' He saw her and gestured impatiently. Then, to her increasing discomfort, he rose from his desk, watching her cross the room, his expression leaving her in no doubt as to what he thought of her appearance. 'Good God! Have *you* been reduced to shopping at jumble sales?'

'No!' she snapped, immediately incensed, not so much by his tactless words, but because she recognised their aptness. 'I haven't,' and, as his eyes narrowed, 'and that doesn't mean I remember, I just know I wouldn't. The thought gives me the creeps. And don't be so personal anyway. My clothes aren't your concern, only my work.'

'I'm sorry. It's just that I don't like to see you ...' He stopped. 'I suppose they *are* your clothes, not Sybil's? She's more generously built than you.'

'I'm told they're mine, and I don't have much choice other than to believe it,' she said with a touch of bitterness. 'Anyway, haven't you anything better to do than to assess women's measurements?' Perhaps he preferred Sybil's figure to hers? She wondered why that idea should occasion her so much pique. She shouldn't care a damn what Tor Endacott thought.

'Yes, I do have better things,' he retorted, 'and if you don't take any pride in your appearance, why should I worry? Here, take a look at these.' He handed her a sheaf of closely written pages. 'See if you can read my writing.'

She skimmed over the notes, wishing she *could* find fault, anything to repay his tactless comments, but his writing, though large, black and sprawling, was well formed and perfectly legible.

'It seems all right,' she admitted grudgingly.

'Right! There's A4 paper and carbons in the desk. Top copy and two carbons, double spacing.' He turned back to his own desk.

Zara sat down and inspected the large typewriter, determined not to ask Tor to explain its mechanics. Finally she inserted the first sheets of paper and began, slowly and cautiously at first, aware that he was watching. She made an error and swore, as she thought, under her breath.

'Correction fluid on the shelf,' the sardonic voice informed her. Why didn't he get on with his own work, instead of sitting there, watching, putting her off.

But as she continued, her confidence increased, until she was keeping up a respectable speed. Tor Endacott's field lay, not in the general topography of the British countryside, but in its folklore. This volume was to cover that of Devon ... celebratory rituals, ghost stories, legends. Zara knew, but again, only by instinct, that this kind of literature was very much to her taste.

It took less time than she'd expected to transform his written words into typescript and she looked across at him, seated at his own desk, auburn head lowered, completely absorbed in his work. The study was warmed by a crackling peat and log fire and Zara felt almost too hot in her thick sweater. Tor was in shirt-sleeves, their cream-coloured silk rolled back to expose muscular forearms, covered in a virile growth of dark hair, and idly Zara found herself wondering how it would feel to run her fingertips over the hair-roughened flesh which still had a healthy summer tan. Maurice's arms and legs, though tanned, were hairless and she felt its possession made Tor appear far more masculine, more virile than the man who was her husband.

The author was in profile to her, his nose, cheekbones and jaw ascetic in their hard, fleshless austerity, yet pleasing to her artistic eye. There! Again this conviction, reinforced now by the information on her marriage lines. She must put the idea to the test, and why not now? Surreptitiously, she began to sketch. The portrait grew rapidly beneath fingers that moved with increasing assurance and she sat back with a feeling of satisfaction, mounting excitement as she compared her work with the original. It was a good likeness. Her marriage certificate had been right about one thing. Her art was certainly of commercial standard. But Tor's gleaming eyes had noticed her surveillance. Quickly she sought to hide the sketch, but he was too swift for her, crossing the room in a few athletic strides, removing the drawing from her suddenly nerveless fingers. He was going to castigate her for wasting time, she thought miserably and sat with bowed head, waiting for the storm to break. Instead, she felt him rest one hand on her shoulder, exerting congratulatory pressure, as, with the other, he returned her sketch.

'This is very good,' he observed, 'but then you . . .' He changed tack and with it his tone. 'I suppose this is another little talent that you just happen to have remembered?'

'Yes!' Smoky-blue eyes met sardonic green ones defiantly. There was no way she was going to tell him about the marriage lines, that his words had prompted her to ask for a sight of it.

'Very strange,' he commented laconically, 'the things you do remember, the things you don't.'

Somehow, despite her uneasiness at his proximity, she found the courage to continue meeting his eyes.

'It may seem odd to you, Mr Endacott, since apparently you know nothing about amnesia. One of the nurses told me about some pop star who even lost his sense of smell and taste . . . had to write down each day's events because nothing would stay in his brain. At least I'm not that bad. All the same,' she ended on a note of despair, 'it's like . . . like living in a black hole.'

'What you're talking about,' he told her, 'is

"short-term amnesia", due to brain damage. It's more common for accident victims, like yourself, to have retrograde amnesia, the inability to recall events which took place before and at the moment of concussion.' He looked at her critically. 'But you don't seem to have suffered from any blows to the head. No bruises. Any lumps?' As he spoke, his lean hands came up to push back the hair from her face, then his fingers were gently probing her scalp, an insidiously pleasant sensation. To her horror, Zara felt an almost irresistible impulse to lean back against him, to relax under his hands, as though it were a caress he inflicted.

Just in time, she remembered that his actions were prompted by scepticism, curiosity, rather than the sensuous urge which suddenly filled *her*. Somewhere, at some time in the past, she had been accustomed to submit to a man's hands stroking her hair in this seductive fashion. No doubt it was her husband's caresses she re-collected. She pulled away, speaking irritably.

'Doing a little amateur phrenology?'

'No,' his deep voice was soft in her ear. 'I don't need to read your bumps to assess your character. It's my guess you're suffering from some form of hysterical amnesia, that for some reason you've blanked out certain events from your mind.'

'You talk as if I did it deliberately.' Angrily she swivelled her chair and pushed with her feet, trundling herself away from those disruptive hands and out of the aura of his male magnetism.

'Subconsciously, you probably did. I wonder,' he added with heavy irony, 'if it's significant that one of the things you can't remember is your marriage?'

'If you're implying that I'd want to forget that, you're crazy!'

'How can you be certain,' he said provocatively, 'when you can't be sure of anything? And why the twin beds?' he said musingly. 'That was Dane's idea, but surely, the most natural thing would be for him to reawaken your memories by making love to you. That's what I'd do, if *I* were your husband.'

It wasn't just Zara's face that flushed. She could feel the whole of her body growing warm ... with indignation at his suggestive manner, she told herself.

'Well, you're *not* my husband and I'd appreciate it if you'd mind your own business.'

'Surely, on the grounds of common humanity, it *is* my business? Wouldn't you attempt anything in your power to help someone in your condition?'

'I don't see how you can help me,' she protested, panic stricken at the thought that he might try to fill his own prescription.

'And you'd object to my trying?' Eyes and voice were twin weapons of seduction and against her will, Zara found herself vibrating responsively.

'I most certainly would! If you dare to lay so much as a finger on me, I'll walk out of here and ...'

'Who said anything about touching you?' he enquired innocently. 'I didn't.'

'You ... you said that Maurice should try ... should try. ...'

'Making love to you? Yes, but then he's your husband, or had you forgotten that again? My remarks were purely academic, but I'm willing to put them into practice if you like. Perhaps you'd rather *I* made love to you?'

'Stop it! Stop it!' Zara put her hands over her ears, shaking her head from side to side. 'I'm confused enough already.' Mortified at having misunderstood him, she felt her eyes filling with the tears which seemed to come so readily since her accident. It was infuriating, since she was almost certain she wasn't the weepy type.

'We could call it an experiment if you like.' he went on. 'A medical experiment.'

'No, we couldn't. *You're* not a doctor.'

'You don't need a degree for what I had in mind,' he purred suggestively. 'It would be interesting, wouldn't it, to see how you respond to another man, when you don't seem to react at all to your own husband.'

'How do you know I don't?' she challenged, anger fast drying the unshed tears. 'You can't possibly know what goes on in the privacy of our room.'

'No?' he drawled. 'Did your husband come to your bed last night, or did you go to his?'

'Look, just what is this ... this inquisition all about? You've no right to intrude on my personal life.' Zara rose, intending to make for the door. 'And I don't have to put up with it.'

'You don't want to answer me, do you?' A long, lean body barred her way. 'Because neither event occurred. You lay alone in your virginal little bed, whilst your husband ...'

'Shut up!' she shouted. 'Shut up, you sadistic brute. Do you get a kick out of torturing people?'

His hand captured hers, before the blow she aimed could find its mark.

'Why?' he probed tormentingly. 'Was it torture, not to be claimed by Dane, by your husband? Did you lie there, in the dark, your body aching to be comforted by his, to be touched, to be possessed?' With each question, despite her struggles, he pulled her closer to him, until her thighs were pressed against his, her back arched, so that he could look down into her flushed, angry face. 'Did you tremble, Zara, with frustrated desire, as you're trembling now?'

'No,' she sobbed, 'because, as you very well know, I don't remember what it's like to be . . . to be . . . He doesn't feel like my husband and . . . and it's not you that's making me . . . making me tremble, or if it is, it's with disgust, n . . . nothing else.'

Again she fought, in a futile attempt to free herself, knowing, despite her denial, that her response was to the insidious male warmth of him. The knowledge was adding to her bewilderment, making her wonder what kind of woman she could be, to feel this tremulous quickening towards a total stranger, when even sharing a room with Maurice, to whom she was married, awoke no similar urgency within her.

'At least not all your emotions are dormant,' Tor observed with clinical satisfaction, his eyes riveted upon her heaving breast. 'You're still capable of anger and you are angry with me, aren't you?'

With him, and with herself. But she couldn't speak, only her eyes glared back her acknowledgement of her fury.

'And if I can rouse you to anger,' he murmured persuasively, 'shouldn't I be able to recall other sensations?' He had overcome all her efforts to escape and now he was crowding her closer, making suggestive little movements of his body against hers, making her heart swing crazily, increasing the confusion that fogged her brain, as she seemed to recall a similar situation, but one in which she had not fought off the seductive advances of a man. This man? Impossible! And yet, for a fraction of a second, it had seemed as if the mists of amnesia would lift, as though she could grasp at a moment of the past, a moment fraught with sensuality. But then, tantalisingly, it evaded her.

'I *know* I could help you, Zara,' he repeated, his head bent, in order to facilitate his mouth's exploration of her neck, the soft skin behind one ear. 'I don't believe that a woman's body can ever forget the sensations of being made love to, whatever tricks her brain might play.'

Frantically, she turned her head from side to side, attempting to dissuade him by kicking his shins.

'What makes you think I should react to *you*?' she managed to demand scornfully. 'You're not my husband. You've never made love to me.'

'No? But perhaps I'd like to.'

'Well, I *wouldn't* like it and I won't let you . . . I . . .'

'What harm could there possibly be in a few kisses? What are you afraid of? That you might remember something, that you're frigid perhaps? What is it that you don't want to remember?' Cruelly, he pressurised her.

'I don't know ... I don't know!' She sobbed for breath. His arms were crushing her to him so tightly that she felt her rib cage could scarcely lift sufficiently to draw in air. 'And I'd *rather* remember. I wouldn't care if I did remember something awful. Anything would be better than this ... this half existence.

'Yes, I think you were made to live life to the full, Zara, so let's see if we can make you live again, hmmn?' His hands began a provocative exploration of her spine, his mouth of her lips.

Some weak part of her was longing to respond to his dominance. She was faint with the sensations he was evoking, so that his lean, tanned features seemed to swim before her eyes, but still she tried to pull herself together. It had suddenly occurred to her that they weren't alone in this house. At any moment Sybil could come in, or Maurice, about his duties, pass the window. What on earth would her husband and her friend think, if they saw her in Tor's arms?

But he was utterly ruthless in his restraint of her and now she couldn't even voice her protest, for his mouth had homed in upon hers, firm, warm, insisting hungrily on the parting of her lips to receive the intimate invasion of his tongue. The kiss was the calculated one of an expert, but, despite her recognition of this fact, it struck hard at her feminine susceptibility. The rough pressure of his mouth, the deep probe of his kiss, sent searing flames of response through her and she realised, with a sense of shock, that she was capable of a sensuality almost equal to his own, that, even if her brain could not, her flesh remembered other moments such as these ... but with whom?

So, she was no iceberg. It was an electrifying discovery. She couldn't hide her instinctive reaction, couldn't hold back the soft surrender of her lips, her body's automatic yielding to his hard, male contours. Vague, nightmarish shapes flitted through her brain, tantalisingly elusive. Were they of recollection or of imagination? She seemed to dwell in a kind of limbo, poised somewhere between the obscurity of the past and the uncertainty of the future. But when his hands loosened their grip of her and began to move over her once more, doing unimaginable things to her tingling nerves, she knew the time had come to call a halt. Whatever his motives, and she didn't believe they were entirely altruistic, it couldn't be right for her to feel this way. However ambiguous her reactions to Maurice, this was disloyalty to her husband and to allow herself to become physically attracted to another man could only pave the way for more uncertainty and heartache.

Fortunately, for she wasn't sure she had the resolution or the physical ability to thrust him away, they were interrupted. Still more fortunately, Sybil knocked before entering and as Tor moved to open the door, Zara gained the sanctuary of the window embrasure, her heated face turned towards the chill, November weather outside.

'I don't know if you stop for coffee?' Sybil enquired and Zara heard Tor exclaim that indeed he did.

'I'd no idea it was that time. Amazing how time flies when you're enjoying your occupation!' This loaded remark, Zara knew, was directed at her, but she dared not turn to scowl at him in

case Sybil noted her flushed cheeks and dis-
hevelled appearance.

At least the arrival of the coffee seemed to have
distracted Tor from his 'experiment', one which
seemed to have left him cool and self-contained,
whereas she . . . She bit her lip. It was going to be
more difficult for *her* to shake off the after-effects
of those kisses, of being in his arms. It must be
her present, peculiarly vulnerable state which
made the circle of his arms seem such a desirable
haven, a source of comfort. Her rationalisation
ignored the fact that, whilst in his arms, safety
and consolation had been the considerations
furthest from her mind.

'You . . . you have a very fine view from this
window,' she said, in an attempt to break the
silence which followed Sybil's departure. 'Is that
some kind of ruin?' She pointed towards what
appeared to be the remains of some ancient castle,
or primitive fortification.

He came to stand behind her, something she
hadn't foreseen when she asked her question, and
she wished he didn't find it necessary to crowd
her so closely, the warmth of him raising the fine
hairs on the nape of her neck, in a prickle of
anticipation. But he didn't touch her.

'That's the Wolfstor, from which the farm
takes its name. A tor is a pointed hill, a granite
outcrop.'

'Is . . . is that where your name came from?'
Zara asked shyly.

'Mmmn. My parents thought it an apt one for
a Dartmoor man.'

'Is it far from here?'

'As the crow flies? No. But don't ever try to

head straight for it. Between us and the Wolfstor
there's the Wolfstor Mire, a certain deathtrap.'

Zara's coffee was finished and she wished he
would stand aside, so she could replace the empty
cup on the tray, but he seemed in no hurry and
though her back was still resolutely turned
towards him, she was certain she could sense his
eyes studying her averted profile. Despite her
own helpless attraction to him, she was shocked
that *he* should have made such open advances to
her. She wasn't naïve. She knew there were
dangers in a man and woman working in close
propinquity, but not, surely, on such short
acquaintance? She wondered how long Tor had
lived here, whether he had been alone for many
months, away from all female companionship.
Was he perhaps starved for . . . for . . .? Her mind
skipped away from the words. Or was he the kind
of man who believed in wasting no time in
preliminaries, if he found a woman desirable?

Probably the latter, she decided. It didn't
improve her opinion of his character. Only the
most unprincipled of men would make love to a
married woman working under his roof, whose
husband moreover was also in his employ. This
disapproval gave Zara the courage she needed to
move past him, trying to ignore the brush of her
body against his.

'Have you any more typing for me?' She made
her voice cool, avoided looking directly at him.

To her relief, he followed her lead and soon she
was immersed in the opening paragraphs of his
first chapter, 'Hauntings on Dartmoor', which
promised hair-raising accounts of spectral ladies,
monks, black dogs and even a pair of large, hairy,

disembodied hands. He only interrupted her once, to ask casually, the unexpected request filling her with elation, whether he might have the sketch of himself to use as the frontispiece of his book.

'Of . . . of course,' she stammered, 'if you really want it. But is it good enough?'

'It's excellent. But if you like, I'll give you a proper sitting.'

'Oh!' To sketch him whilst he was unaware was one thing, but she floundered at the prospect of having to study his face whilst he sat there, aware of her gaze, perhaps in his turn assessing *her* features.

'Think about it,' he recommended, 'if you feel you haven't done your talent justice and would like to try another version.'

What could she say? To refuse would sound like conceit, as if she deemed herself capable of perfection at first attempt.

'I . . . I'd like to try again,' she said at last.

'One evening then?' he suggested. 'There's very little to do here on a winter's night. One has to make one's own amusements.'

Why did this final phrase fill her with unease? Did the suggestion that she perfect her portrait cover some ulterior motive?

The rest of the morning passed swiftly for Zara, absorbed in Tor's detailing of legends, and as a gong from the kitchen regions announced lunch, she rose and stretched, her shoulders stiff with the prolonged, unaccustomed hours of typing. Movements that on her part were purely reflex caught Tor's eye and she straightened swiftly, suddenly aware that, despite the unflattering bagginess of her sweater, the arching of her back and shoulders had brought the generous curves of her breasts into prominence. She moved towards the door, intent on reaching the safety of other company, but his movements were as swift and he detained her, one hand above her head, preventing the door from opening.

'How have you enjoyed your first morning?' The question was innocently phrased, but from the glint in his eyes, she knew it was heavily loaded, that he wasn't just referring to the typing. Purposely, she chose to misunderstand.

'I found the work very enjoyable.'

'And how about the "therapy"? Did it produce any results? Recall any forgotten . . . sensations?' He sounded so perfectly certain that his tactics must have produced results that Zara was driven to deflate his pretensions.

'Sorry to disappoint you. I'm afraid your "treatment" left me quite cold.' She was lying, at least about the effect. His calculated lovemaking had achieved very definite effects upon her senses, even if it hadn't cleared her mind, and he *knew* that she lied.

'Not to worry,' he told her and with a wickedly mocking smile, 'just keep taking the medicine.'

For a moment she stared at him. She wasn't on any medication. Then the penny dropped.

'If you think I'm going to allow any repetition . . .'

'So how do you intend to prevent it?' he asked interestedly. 'We shall be working together, closely, for weeks, months even, in this room and somehow I don't think you're going to persuade your husband to take you away from here. I don't even think you're going to tell him about this morning, are you, Zara?' Lean fingers came out and entrapped her chin, lifting her face so he could study her furious, mutinous expression. 'Are you?' he repeated.

Lids lowered against his probing gaze, she shook her head, though it galled her to do so.

'You know I can't,' she whispered. 'He needs this job. It wouldn't be fair and . . . and besides, I don't know how he'd react.'

'Yes, he needs this job.' Tor repeated her statement with strange emphasis and she looked up enquiringly. Did he know something about Maurice that she didn't? How could he? They hadn't met until yesterday. 'Of course I suppose you might confide my outrageous behaviour to your friend?'

'No!' She couldn't see herself confiding anything to Sybil, still couldn't think how this woman came to be an intimate friend.

'No?' Again he was mocking her. 'But I thought you were so close that you couldn't bear to be parted, even though you're now a married woman? Why do you think you'd want a third party to your marriage? Is it some sort of kinky triangle?'

'Don't be so . . . so disgusting!' Outraged, she stamped her foot and then gloated as he winced. Accidentally, with her angry gesture, she had located his toes.

'Then I can only assume you didn't want to be alone with Dane. I wonder why?'

'Mr Endacott! Will you stop this . . . this ill-mannered prying! I want my lunch. Sybil sounded the gong ages ago, She'll be wondering . . .'

To her relief, he relaxed his pressure on the door and with sarcastic politeness held it open for her.

'By all means let's eat first. You're allowed a full hour before I'll want you to take up . . . er . . . where we left off.'

She eyed him suspiciously. Was he referring to the transcription of his manuscript, or . . .? As she made to precede him from the study, his hand closed over a thick tress of her hair, halting her, as he bent his head in a swift, light caress of her lips, against which he murmured:

'You'll just have to wait and see, won't you?'

CHAPTER THREE

But, as if he felt he'd spent enough time on Zara's rehabilitation, Tor worked with zeal that afternoon, the words flowing from his pen nearly as fast as Zara could type them. He'd been silent over lunch, but she'd noticed his eyes going from one to another of their trio and she didn't think his gaze had rested any longer on her than on Sybil or Maurice. Just what *did* he make of their strange *ménage à trois*? She didn't really know what to make of it herself. Her own feelings apart, it took a very forbearing husband to agree to the inclusion of another woman in his household.

'I'd better assume,' Tor told her, when they paused to take a tea-break, 'that you know nothing about Dartmoor. Just remember that it's not an area you can take liberties with, particularly at this time of year. The weather can be atrocious and it can kill. Fog is the worst enemy. It's easy to lose your way and your head. You can walk straight into a mire or a bog, often with fatal results. So if you get a yen to go exploring, seek the company of someone experienced.'

'Such as yourself?' She couldn't help the sarcastic note.

'Yes,' he answered quite seriously. 'I've lived most of my life around here.'

'And do you subscribe to its superstitions too?'

Her question was a frivolous one, but again he chose to answer her literally.

'I don't fear them,' he said slowly, 'but neither do I discount them. Only the foolish reject something which can neither be proved nor disproved. The moor has its terrors and it's only prudent to be aware of them.'

'You actually believe there could be such things? This black huntsman you've written about?'

'I don't think it's wise to deny the existence of evil, the devil, call it what you will, and it's said that Dewer *is* the devil, hunting all night across the moorland with his black hellhounds. You'll find, if you ever read my other books, that all wild places have eerie qualities ascribed to Old Nick.'

'I would quite like to read some of your books . . . if only to pass the time,' she added, in case he suspected her of flattery.

'Help yourself, whenever you feel the need.' He indicated a row of shelves lining one wall. 'But do,' he added with the ghost of a smile, 'tell me, if you should find time hanging heavily on your hands. I'm sure I'll be able to think of some occupation for them.' Before she could decide how to take this comment, he added: 'And how about you? Are you prey to superstition, of a nervous disposition?'

'I don't think so,' Zara's brow wrinkled attractively, 'though I must admit I wouldn't like to be out there alone at night.'

'Superstition and weather apart, it isn't wise to be alone on the moor at any time. It isn't a common occurrence, fortunately, but there's always a chance of a breakout from the prison.

You do know we're quite close to Princetown, I suppose?' His gaze was suddenly intent.

'Yes. How do the people round here feel about having dangerous men so close?'

'Somewhat mixed. You can't help being sorry for the poor devils. It's one of the grimmest prisons in existence and there's been talk of closing it down. But sympathy goes out of the window when the sirens sound and there's a chance of encountering an inmate.'

'Would people harbour an escaped prisoner? Would *you*?'

'No, I most certainly would not! So if you ever meet one, don't bring him here!' It was said jestingly, but a certain seriousness underlying his words made her wonder a little.

That evening, Tor suggested she begin his portrait. Zara hadn't anticipated so immediate a request and she fumbled for excuses.

'I don't have any proper drawing paper, or pens. I like a special draughtsman's pen for ...' She stopped, her blue-grey eyes huge as she met Tor's suddenly fixed gaze. 'That's a memory, isn't it?' she asked him excitedly. 'It just came into my mind.'

'So you say.'

'Yes, I do say,' she snapped. 'I should have thought you'd be glad my memory seems to be improving.'

'I don't know about that,' he drawled, 'since then there'd be no necessity for any "treatment" on my part!'

'That won't be necessary in any case,' she told him sharply. 'I'd rather recover naturally, in my own time.'

'As it happens,' he returned to the subject of the sketch, 'we do have materials to hand. I *was* expecting a very fine artist to illustrate the legends for me. I'd laid in all the necessary pens and papers, but I was let down.'

'What will you do?' she asked.

'I don't know. One can't photograph mystery and imagination. Find someone else, I suppose.' His smile teased her. 'Who knows, perhaps we'll find your work is up to standard?'

'Oh!' Instead of rising to the bait, after all, she now knew she *was* a draughtswoman, she stared raptly at him. 'Mr Endacott, do you *mean* it? I should enjoy that and ... and I have a feeling I could do it.'

'I bet you do!' he said obscurely. Had *he* been questioning Maurice about her past? 'Let's just wait and see what you make of the portrait before we get too carried away.'

Sybil and Maurice were in the comfortable living-room, listening to the radio. Wolfstor didn't boast a television set. Zara allowed them to think, and Tor didn't contradict, that they would be working on his book. She was wary yet of revealing to them her rediscovered skills. Besides, she didn't like anyone to see a drawing until it was complete. Again she was awed by the way these little snippets of information were slowly seeping back into her mind.

'I often play music when I'm working,' Tor said, putting on a record, 'but you may not find my kind of music particularly soothing.'

And, as she listened, she found his choice somewhat disturbing, full of an eerie weirdness which accorded well with his choice of a home,

the subject matter of his books; Carl Orff's
'Carmina Burana', wild, exciting, primitive, with
strong overtones of sexuality. Yet it seemed to
draw from her fingers the very impression she
wished to convey, strong assured lines leaping
out upon the paper, bringing out the primitive
male, which she sensed lay beneath the cultured
veneer, the deceptively ascetic lineaments of his
face. '*Fortuna Imperatrix Mundi*', Fortune, Ruler
of the World, was the title of the opening
movement, and Tor, Zara felt, was very much
ruler of this bleak, isolated world in which he
chose to live.

She put the finishing touches to her sketch and
with a flourish signed her name, 'Zara'. She felt
no compulsion to add the 'Dane' or any other, as
though her first name only was her usual signa-
ture to her work. Another 'memory' on which to
ponder? Tor took the work.

'Yes,' he said with satisfaction, 'this *is* even
better. Whatever's become of your memory, you
certainly haven't lost your touch. How much do
you want for it?'

'H ... how much?' She'd done the drawing as
much to satisfy her curiosity as to the extent of
her abilities, as to please Tor.

'This is a very professional piece of work and
the labourer is worthy of her hire.'

'But I didn't expect ... I mean ...'

'*Would* you like to illustrate my book, Zara?'

'You really mean it, don't you?' she said
wonderingly.

'I generally say what I mean. We'd have to come
to some financial agreement of course. Well?' His
decision made, he was impatient for hers.

'I'd like that very much, but what about the typing?'

'I don't believe it would tax you too much to do both. And it would more than double your salary.'

'Maurice will be pleased.'

'You surely won't be handing over your salary to him?' Tor said sharply. 'Good Lord, girl, your earning power is far greater than his.'

'I don't know,' she admitted, 'I hadn't thought about it. If we ever discussed any arrangements I suppose I've forgotten. I just naturally assumed . . .'

'I shall pay you separately for your artwork,' Tor said decisively. 'It has nothing to do with your three-way arrangement. Let them think all your time is spent on typing my manuscript.'

'I don't like the idea of deceiving my husband.'

'I can't think how Dane ever came to *be* your husband.' Tor threw out the statement with such conviction that Zara could only stare. Besides, she couldn't protest, when she'd wondered the same thing once or twice herself in the last twenty-four hours. 'You're totally mismatched,' he continued, 'what did you see in him?'

'I'd rather not discuss it,' she said stiffly, 'it's very unfair to Maurice. Since I can't remember anything about our marriage, I'm not in a position to defend him as I could if I . . .'

'No way!' he said positively. 'When you regain your memory, I'm confident you'll find it was all one big mistake.'

'Don't say that, please,' she begged brokenly, the colour of her eyes deepening tragically. 'My life feels uncertain enough. Don't take away my only shred of security.'

'Zara! Zara!' he chided, drawing her up from where she sat, giving her an admonitory shake. 'Someone like you doesn't need the no-hopers of this world, like Dane. Take it from me, your artwork would earn you a living anywhere. I'll tell you what! When you decide to get rid of him, *I'll* employ you on a permanent basis.'

'I thought we *were* employed permanently.' She ignored his half-jesting manner.

Tor shook his head slightly, his eyes consideringly upon the perfect oval of her face.

'This job will only last three months at the outside.'

She felt a little surge of disappointment. She would be here for such a short while, involved in Tor's work so briefly.

'Is that your idea?' she asked. 'Or . . .'

'Mutual really. Wolfstor is my home, but I travel around a lot, so it isn't economical to keep it open all year. I generally come home for autumn and winter, then go touring in spring and summer. Eventually I hope to extend my travels to Europe, revisit some of the places where I worked years ago, But in any case, when your husband took the job, he said it would suit him perfectly to be employed just for the three months.' He looked closely at Zara. 'I'm surprised he hasn't reminded you of that. Not much communication between you, is there?'

'Perhaps it just didn't occur to him,' Zara said defensively, then: 'What did you mean when you called him a "no-hoper"?'

He shrugged, releasing his hold on her shoulders as he did so, and a chill emptiness seemed to fill the place where the warmth of his hands had been, making Zara shiver as at a deprivation.

'Someone unqualified, with no particular profession or ambition, who'll never do more than scrape a living.'

Zara digested this in silence. Tor seemed to know more about her husband than she did. How on earth *had* she got involved with someone like that? She felt certain that any man in her life would have to command her respect. How could she have fallen for the type Tor described?

'Doesn't make sense, does it?' Tor said.

She didn't waste time asking what he meant. She'd already encountered this uncanny knack of his of reading her mind. She looked at her wristwatch.

'Hadn't we better join the others? They may think it strange if we're in here all hours of the day and night.'

'Afraid your husband may get jealous?' he mocked.

'He'd have reason, if he knew how you'd behaved this morning.'

'But we decided you wouldn't tell him?'

'Yes, but don't count on my silence if you try anything like that again.'

He made no comment, but one eyebrow lifted sardonically and she knew Tor was impervious to threats. He motioned her towards the door and as she preceded him, reminded her of his offer.

'To *you* I *would* offer permanent employment.'

'You can't. You won't be here.'

'Secretaries often travel with their employers and if you're going to be my illustrator too . . .'

To travel around the British Isles, perhaps

further afield, with Tor as her companion! Zara drew in her breath at the evocative thought. No more alluring employment could ever be offered to her, but the *employer*! It was totally impossible. If he'd been the elderly professor she'd envisaged, it might have been feasible, with no risk to her marriage. But she couldn't see Maurice countenancing such an arrangement, nor herself being able to maintain a platonic relationship with Tor. She'd already received striking proof of her susceptibility to him and she had the feeling he would always be one to make the most of any opportunities that came his way . . . in her case, under the guise of helping her recover her memory.

'It's out of the question,' she said decidedly, but aware of a pang that smote her somewhere beneath her ribcage at the thought of all she was refusing, the job *and* Tor's company, she realised. But he seemed undeflated.

'Don't make any hasty decisions. A lot can happen in three months. I can afford to play a waiting game.'

With this cryptic remark, he ushered her out of the study and they rejoined the others, the conversation becoming general, and Tor exerted himself to be particularly charming to Sybil.

Zara, attempting to act naturally with her husband, as much for Tor's benefit as for any other reason, found herself trying to listen to two conversations at once. It was all right for Sybil, she thought, *she* wasn't tied. She *could* respond to Tor's subtle flattery, return his badinage without pangs of conscience.

Horrified, she realised just how resentful she

was of being married, of Maurice's presence, his existence even. She was jealous of Sybil, her freedom and, above all, the attention Tor was paying her! With an abrupt excuse that she was tired, she rose, announcing her intention of going to bed.

A wicked glint in Tor's eyes, almost as though he suspected her motives, presaged mischief.

'I suppose that means we'll be losing your company too, Dane? Since newly-weds have a propensity for retiring early!'

A dull, brick-red colour crept up under Maurice's tan, but he answered civilly and although it obviously hadn't been his intention, he rose to escort Zara.

Because her plea of weariness had not been genuine, but an excuse to escape the sight of Tor flirting with Sybil, Zara was not really tired and she lay awake for some time, listening to the muted sound of voices and laughter below, wondering what they were talking about, hearing them grow louder, as Tor and Sybil mounted the stairs together, still in companionable conversation. Then she heard the distinct closing of two separate doors and the reassuring sound seemed to release her tension. Pleasantly drowsy at last, she snuggled down, only to be disturbed again, this time by sounds nearer at hand, from the adjacent bed. As on the previous night, Maurice had slipped out, a silent shadow, and this time Zara did not fall asleep, but found herself waiting for his return.

He didn't come back and after a while curiosity drew her from her bed and out on to the landing. There was no sign of Maurice, but a light shone beneath Sybil's door and there was a low murmur of voices. Without considering her motives, Zara tiptoed along the landing.

As she drew nearer, one of the voices rose in anger. Not Tor, then? Had she really been so anxious that it shouldn't be? But what on earth was Maurice doing in Sybil's room? Strangely she felt no sense of outrage, only extreme curiosity.

'How do *I* know what you get up to in there?' Sybil's harsh voice rose too and this time Maurice pleaded moderation.

'Remember *he's* only next door and he's nobody's fool.'

'Quite a man, isn't he?' This was said with a throaty chuckle.

'Watch it, Syb, don't play games with me. I noticed how willing you were to stay downstairs with him.'

'O.K., O.K. Just joking. But listen, are you quite certain she's not faking this amnesia? She's a cunning little bitch. I wouldn't put it past her to try and spike our guns even now. If only he hadn't insisted we brought her along ...' If who hadn't insisted, Zara puzzled? 'If I had my way ...'

'It may come to that yet,' Maurice said grimly. The sound of his footsteps approaching the door sent Zara scuttling for cover, but she had heard enough to convince her that Maurice was having an affair with Sybil. Odd that it should affect her so little.

So why had Maurice married her instead of Sybil and how long did he intend to keep up their three-sided relationship? Could that be what their argument had been about, the argument preceding her car crash? Perhaps she'd discovered his unfaithfulness?

Zara had expected that the next day would follow much the same pattern as the first, but Tor had other ideas. Instead of handing her the anticipated sheaf of notes for transcription, he told her to fetch a warm coat.

'Ideally, you could do with wearing slacks,' he said, with a disparaging glance at the shapeless grey skirt, worn today with a sweater in an electric blue as hideous as the previous day's green.

'I haven't any,' she informed him, and after a pause, in which he seemed to deliberate, he ordered:

'Come with me!'

Wonderingly, she followed him upstairs, into the spare bedroom, where he threw open a wardrobe, displaying several items of female attire, among which was a serviceable pair of denim jeans.

'Put these on,' he commanded, 'and while you're here, feel free to use any of these clothes,' and, as she demurred, 'The owner won't be needing them any longer, and they're only taking up space.'

Zara was tempted. The clothes weren't new, but they *were* well made, about the right size too, the colours more to her taste. Who had owned them? One of Tor's ex-girlfriends? She shrugged fatalistically. It was none of her business how many women had stayed here and left behind their cast-off clothing, and she couldn't afford to be choosy. Nevertheless, she stored up the suspicion for future reference.

She carried off her spoils and ten minutes later, far more at ease in these borrowed clothes, which might almost have been made for her, she followed Tor out into the rear yard.

'You asked yesterday about Dewer, the black huntsman,' he explained. 'I thought you might care to see the area he's reputed to haunt, make a few sketches?'

Zara nodded her dark head eagerly. This chance of illustrating Tor's legendary tales was a much-needed lifeline, not only as a boost to her self-confidence, but as a link that stretched back into the past, that some day might prove to be the key to the barrier dividing the two compartments of her life.

She'd expected an author of Tor's stature to have a large, expensive car, but the vehicle, a foreign model, was the smallest she'd ever seen, a bright, cheerful, red ladybird of a car, into which it seemed almost impossible two adults could fit. They managed it, however, even though Zara felt it brought her into uncomfortably close proximity with the driver.

In these confined conditions, she was very aware of Tor. Once his hand brushed her knee as he changed gear, and she sat well over to the left, pretending an absorption in the scenery which soon became genuine.

As far as the eye could see, great ridges of brown heathland lay silent, a true wilderness, lonely, bare, cruel-looking. Lofty granite tors lifted jagged edges to the sky, though none were quite as imposing as that which gave the farmhouse its name. Wolfstor, her companion told her, was visible from almost any point in a circumference of several miles, handy if one were lost.

'I can see how this place might suit your style of writing,' she told him, 'it's almost fey.'

The heights of Dartmoor were virtually treeless, but Wistman's Wood, their destination, was an upland copse that had survived from ancient times, its individual trees being oaks, stunted, twisted and gnarled into fantastic shapes.

'Like a wood in a fairy tale,' Zara breathed, urgent to capture the crazy grotesque lines on paper. 'Can't you just imagine those branches as evil, twisted arms?'

'According to local legend, it's this wood that's haunted by the Wild Hunt, where, if you're out late enough at night, you'll hear the sound of the Dark Huntsman's horn and the fierce cries of his hounds.'

Zara was already absorbed, sketchbook in hand, making studies of roots, branches and twigs, of the great, grey boulders.

'I'll work this into a proper drawing this evening,' she promised, as she looked up at him, smoky-blue eyes afire with enthusiasm. 'Oh, Mr Endacott, I'm going to enjoy this.'

'Why not call me "Tor"?' He came to sit beside her, among the gnarled roots, those strange green eyes viewing with interest the colour that rose in her cheeks. 'I call you Zara,' he pointed out.

'I . . . I . . .' Her fingers clenched so tightly around her pencil that the point snapped. 'Oh . . . and I haven't another with me.'

'Forget the pencil!' He took it and thrust it into his pocket, and her sketchbook followed. He rose to his feet, drawing her with him. Steadfastly she gazed down at her feet, aware that her colour was deepening, the heat seeming to encompass the whole of her body, aware that this situation was fraught with possibilities she was incapable of avoiding. A determined hand forced up her chin.

'Say it! Say my name!'

With a sudden spurt of irritation at his autocratic manner, she managed to stare straight into those disconcerting eyes.

'Very well! Tor, if you insist.'

'I *do* insist,' he said softly, 'just as I'm about to insist on kissing those pouting, rebellious lips of yours.'

She backed off, resisting, even though she knew, with rising shame, that she wanted Tor to kiss her. But she wasn't capable of holding him at bay. The threatened kiss came, gently, teasingly at first, inviting her response. Sternly, she fought the insidious desire to respond. She mustn't allow herself to become involved with Tor. She freed her lips.

'Have you forgotten I'm married?'

'Has *Maurice* forgotten that?' he retorted, then, as she stared at him, 'It *was* his voice I heard in Sybil's room last night?'

'I . . . I don't know what you mean,' she denied.

'Really?' His drawl was sardonic. 'I suppose you were too occupied with your pretty little ear glued to the door to notice that I opened mine fractionally, to see what was going on?'

Zara flushed scarlet. To be caught unintentionally eavesdropping was bad enough, but for Tor to know that Maurice was unfaithful to her, a bride of only a few weeks, was humiliating.

'I . . . I didn't have my ear against the door and . . . and . . . they probably had business to discuss,' she invented wildly.

'What business could be so important as to take him to her room in the middle of the night? Come off it, Zara,' his tone was cynical, 'Dane was in that room for fully two hours, during most of which time there was very little conversation.'

'So I wasn't the only one eavesdropping,' she snapped.

'Of course not.' His lips brushed a soft line across her temple. 'Didn't I *tell* you, sweetheart, that I had your interests at heart?'

She tried to ignore the effect upon her of that murmured endearment, tried to jerk out of reach of the warm, seductive mouth.

'I don't see how you think it will help, to tell me.'

'But you didn't need telling, you already knew. I wonder how long their little affair has been going on? Since your accident, or long before? You must be slipping, Zara,' he taunted.

Without weighing the consequences of her actions, she attacked him, using every weapon at her disposal, fists, feet, fingernails, even teeth. But she was no match for his tensile strength. Easily he held her at bay, openly laughing at her puny efforts, until she burst into tears of frustrated anger. Then his manner altered, face and hands softening, as he drew her, unresisting now, back into his arms.

'Poor little waif,' he murmured against her hair, 'you've no one to turn to really, have you? You don't know who to trust, husband, friend . . .'

'And I can't trust you either,' she sobbed, clinging to him nevertheless, 'all *you* do is accuse me of faking my amnesia, or if you're not doing that you're . . . you're trying to . . . to seduce me.'

'Zara!' He sounded deeply shocked, the hypocrite! 'All *I* want to do is to help you remember.'

'You've a strange way of helping people,' she hiccuped. 'Why don't you just bang me on the head? It couldn't be more painful than what you're doing to me. Isn't that supposed to restore memory?'

'In very hackneyed fiction, perhaps, but I don't see myself striking a woman. Personally,' his voice became insinuative, 'I prefer the gentle touch.'

He began a very practical demonstration, his long, sensitive fingers slowly, sensuously exploring her throat, unzipping her quilted jacket to seek the wool of her sweater, beneath which his hands slipped with smooth assurance, seeking the warm flesh beneath.

Forced against the uneven bole of a twisted oak, Zara was unaware of its uncomfortable pressure on her spine, as his thighs moulded hers and his lips tasted away the salty tears of her distress, then moved to her mouth, demandingly persistent, drawing a response from her as primitive as the ancient wood within which they stood. The deepening kiss caused her to cling shudderingly to him, responding, as hungry as he now for closer contact.

His kiss banished all pangs of conscience, erased all her indignation with him, consoled her misery, bewitched her senses, conjuring up behind her rapturously closed eyes drowned memories, scenes of herself held fast in the arms of a tall man, whose kisses moved her to a groaning need like this, a man whose face she must see. But still it eluded her and a great sigh of frustration racked her. It was exquisite torture to feel that her body, her lips remembered an unattainable paradise where her mind could not follow.

But to have allowed him to kiss her like this was a terrible mistake. Now that she knew her own potential for flaring passion, would she ever be able to temper her longing for him? She had tried so hard not to allow herself to be moved by Tor's masculinity. But was it to him she responded, or was he just the catalyst to arouse deeply buried, nebulous dreams of love and physical fulfilment, coalescing fragments of the past as, she realised with sudden shock, he had planned to do? So was it to him or to the shadowy lover his kisses evoked and was that shadow her husband? If so, she had no right to be giving the responses that were his to Tor Endacott.

She attempted to push him away, fought to restrain caressing, seductive hands that were rousing her flesh to soaring peaks of promised ecstasy. But if Tor's lovemaking had begun as a therapeutic experiment, there was no doubt now that his body had usurped the functions of his brain. All other motives seemingly forgotten, he surged against her, with all the pent up strength of his own arousal, his desire as deeply stirred as hers.

With the ancient tree as his ally, he had her trapped, a long, muscular leg entwined with hers, its thrust deliberate provocation, and she couldn't disguise an involuntary shudder of pleasure. Even her lips were denied their right of protest, for he held them enslaved by his.

Slowly, carefully, making sure that the contact between them was not broken for an instant, he took them both down to the woodland floor, its crisp, autumn covering dampened by November mists, a soft couch for their trembling, urgent bodies.

CHAPTER FOUR

'Soon you'll remember what it's like,' he groaned huskily against her ear, his hands moving with assurance on the zip of her borrowed jeans.

'No!' she gasped, sanity gaining ascendance. She didn't want to remember *this* way, to have Tor's lovemaking remind her of another man's possession. What if returning memory should bring the knowledge that hers was a loveless marriage, that the ecstasy Tor offered her could only result in a different kind of torture? She wasn't free to love him and to him this was only an exercise, in which he pitted his male allure against the hold that shock had established over her mind.

She wrestled with him, no longer half-heartedly, but with a kind of despairing determination that produced unexpected reserves of strength.

'Let me go!' She sought for words to reinforce her actions. 'Only animals behave like this.'

'Prefer the cover of darkness, do you?' he mocked. 'I don't believe you, Zara.' His breath came unevenly, as he sought with hard hands, with the weight of his lean, muscular body, to subdue her angry writhings.

'Well, I do,' she snapped, 'and I'd also prefer a different man!'

Her words achieved their effect. He released her, pushing himself upright in one angry jerk, leaving her spread-eagled among the damp leaves.

'What exactly does *that* mean?' he snarled, jaw working spasmodically, as he fought to bring his own physical reactions under control.

'Just what I said.' She scrambled to her feet. 'I *won't* play around outside of marriage.'

'Even though your husband doesn't abide by the same rules?'

'Perhaps that's my fault,' she said quietly, 'perhaps up to now I haven't made sufficient effort.'

'And is that what you intend to do?' he asked, his features drawing into cold, hard lines, 'even though you can't remember the fellow from Adam? Damn it, Zara! It's immoral!'

'Is it?' she flashed. 'Would it be more "moral" of me to have sex with you? Whether I remember or not doesn't matter. I'm married to Maurice and there's no law that says I can't make love to my own husband.'

She turned and began to walk back to the car, conscious of him striding behind her in simmering silence. She would be glad when the return journey was over. The tiny interior of the car seemed loaded with atmosphere. Tor spoke only once, tautly.

'And when do you plan to put this ... this campaign into action?'

Zara had no such plans, but she didn't intend to tell him that.

'Why not tonight?' She injected a note of sweet reason into her voice. 'The sooner the better, surely?'

He growled an unspeakable word and the

gearbox grated harshly as he changed down for a bend.

Over the next few days, Zara was conscious that she and Maurice were being closely watched, by two pairs of eyes, Sybil's and Tor's. What they wouldn't give to be able to see into our room, she thought wryly. To Tor she contrived to give the impression of quiet contentment, one which roused him to a gnawing irritability. The only things which seemed to please him were her drawings.

One afternoon Tor had gone into Tavistock on business, and with no manuscript to type, Zara grew restless. There would be a couple of hours of daylight before the wintry day drew to a close. She would take her sketchblock out on to the moor. There was a particular setting she needed for one of the more supernatural tales.

She found her location, and as she settled herself on a convenient projection of rock, she heard a low, distant rumble of thunder. At this time of year? But Tor had said Dartmoor weather was unpredictable and besides the storm was too far away to trouble *her*. Absorbed in her sketch, she didn't notice the sky gradually become more overcast, the great black clouds coming nearer to where she sat, the gloom shutting out the thin, lemon-pale winter sunshine. It was the first few heavy drops of rain spattering her sketchpad which alerted her to the need to seek shelter.

Another burst of large raindrops was followed by a tremendous peal of thunder, beneath whose shock the moorland seemed to quiver, distant hills and tors re-echoing its warning roar. A vivid flash of lightning split the ink-black clouds, seeming to bounce off nearby rocks. Land of Thunder, she thought, with almost a sense of exhilaration, the old name for Dartmoor.

Thrusting her sketchpad inside her coat to protect her drawing, Zara lowered her head against the elements, which now beat upon her with full fury, and began to stumble homeward. Soon she was cursing herself for wandering so far. There was no other building between her and the farm.

Blinded by sheeting rain, she couldn't see any track and she knew she was lost when she reached a stream she hadn't passed before. Already swollen by rain, overflowing its banks, there was no dry crossing to be had. Fatalistically, since she was soaked anyway, she waded through the water.

The storm was lessening, but it was dark now and her landmark, the Wolfstor, was no longer visible. 'The moor can kill,' Tor had warned her. Suppose she stumbled into a mire, to be sucked down into some watery morass.

New terrors came to her in the sound of hoofbeats, a flashing light that rose and fell. All the tales she had typed, of ghostly horsemen, returned to haunt her. But it was no phantom voice that called her name and with a sob of relief, she stumbled forward, calling out the rider's name in weary gratitude.

With rescue at hand, reaction set in and with a loud oath, Tor drew his mount to a halt by her crumpled figure, his relief finding vent in violent anger.

'You stupid, bloody little fool! What are you

trying to do, commit suicide?' Regardless of the mud, he was on his knees, anger lapsing into concern as he lifted her soaked, inert form.

'It's all right,' she assured him weakly. 'I haven't fainted, it's just that my legs are so tired and ... oh, Tor,' she gave a little gulp, 'I'm so glad to see you.' It seemed natural to snuggle her head against his shoulder.

'See me! That's rich, in this muck!' But he didn't sound angry now, though the emotion was just as intense. 'Zara, you are without doubt ... God, can you imagine my feelings when we realised you must have gone out on the moor, and then the storm broke. Do you realise what might have happened to you?'

'Yes,' she admitted meekly, then sighed contentedly. 'But I'm safe now you're here.'

'I wouldn't be too sure about *that*,' he told her, as his mingled relief and fury found vent in a sudden brutal assault upon her lips, as though to punish her for the anxiety she'd caused him.

Wet and cold, nevertheless Zara felt a familiar, insistent stirring in her blood under the harsh stimulation of his mouth. To respond seemed as natural as breathing and his hold on her tightened urgently. There was no need for him to prise her lips apart, already they had softened, opening eagerly for his invasion and her arms went around his neck, her hands finding the thick hair, slicked smooth by the torrential rain through which he'd ridden ... to find *her*. He must care about her safety, she thought exultantly, to take such a risk himself.

At the thought, her mouth moved invitingly under his, giving a sensuous reply to his own. He shuddered, his hold upon her intensifying, their uncomfortable conditions ignored in this mutual surge of passion.

Absorbed in each other, they scarcely noticed the resumption of the thunder, until a final shattering peal sent her jerking with fear in his arms. But Tor seemed not to heed the elemental warning, his emotions in accord with its violence he covered her, coming between her and the threat from above, his urgent body not so much a protection now, as a warning of dangers just as real as those from natural forces.

The storm was within her too, firing her blood, she was possessed by a pleasure that forked as violently, as explosively, as the lightning, splitting the darkened sky. The thunder was the beating of her own heart. Feverishly, her hands caressed and moulded his hair and face, her body arched to meet and experience the pulsating movements of his.

At first she didn't understand the murmured question, drowned as it was by the sounds around them. He repeated his words.

'I want you, Zara . . . *you* want *me* . . .'

Shocked into sanity, she jack-knifed away from him, striving to regulate her breathing, to still the traitorous quiverings of her body, as she rejected his statement. His voice was harsh, unsteady, self-deriding, as he rose, pulling her to her feet.

'I seem doomed to failure with my experiment . . and don't say you're sorry,' he commanded savagely, 'don't say anything at all. My God, if you knew what you've just done to me!' So impassioned was his manner, that she feared he might try to hold her to him again and purposely she injected scornful surprise into her voice.

'I wasn't *going* to apologise, except for the inconvenience I've caused you, bringing you out in this weather. In fact, I think *you're* the one who should apologise for . . . for . . .' She backed away as his sudden movement seemed to threaten her.

'Oh, don't worry!' he snapped. 'I've suddenly realised that I'm freezing cold, wet and thoroughly turned off.'

When Zara came to translate the sodden but still recognisable sketch into a masterpiece, every line was accompanied by insidious memories of those moments following her rescue, and she knew that, for ever afterwards, the sight of the picture would evoke for her Tor's elemental passion. For his part, he made no further reference to the incident and seemed totally absorbed in his work. After several weeks of his cool, matter-of-fact politeness, Zara began to think he'd lost interest in his attempts to rehabilitate her . . . had lost interest in her too.

There were often days when Tor left her to work alone, and he gave no explanations for these increasingly frequent absences, except for the occasion when he stated he was going into the nearest large town, to stock up on essential supplies. Forecasts for the area, he explained, were deteriorating. At the very least, fog would come down on the moor, lasting many days, making motoring hazardous if not downright impossible. They were already cut off enough, Zara considered, with no telephone, an instrument to which Tor had strong objections. It was a time-waster, he maintained, something liable to interrupt the flood of inspiration.

He'd left Zara sufficient material to keep her occupied and at first she worked hard, absorbed as usual in his stories, But, about mid-morning, she began to flag. Normally, she and Tor broke off for a coffee, but no one had bothered to bring her a drink this morning. She made her way along the flagged passageway that linked the front of the house with the kitchen, then hesitated at the sound of raised voices.

'I'm getting brassed off with this existence.' It was Sybil, harsh, shrewish. 'We do all the hard work, while Madam Zara sits about on her bottom, and you have to creep about at night like a burglar to get to my room.'

'Look, love,' Maurice was trying to placate the angry woman, 'I know it's not easy, but it shouldn't be for much longer and once this is all over, it'll be back to dear old Aussie and the good life for us.'

'I wish we'd never left,' Sybil commented bitterly.

'You know we had to,' Maurice pleaded, 'we couldn't let him down and when we found out what had happened, we had to stay.'

Who was this mysterious 'he' the couple were always speaking of. Somehow Zara didn't think it could be Tor . . . and yet who else was there?

'Well, I just hope he'll show his gratitude, that's all . . . and there's another thing, what are we going to do about Madam Zara, afterwards?'

Zara tensed, moving closer to the door.

'That's for him to decide.'

'She could get her memory back at any moment,' Sybil pointed out, 'and then we'd really be in the soup. Suppose she got it back when she was somewhere we couldn't get at her.'

Zara's knees were beginning to feel decidedly wobbly. There was so much venom in Sybil's tone. Instead of hoping for her recovery, Sybil and Maurice seemed terrified that she *would* regain her memory.

'If she'd got away from us that time,' Sybil continued, 'she'd have spilt the beans to the first policeman she met. Everything would have been ruined, and it could still happen.'

Zara shuddered, but she knew it was vital for her to go on listening. What knowledge lay in her subconscious that these two feared? Her amnesia had never been more frustrating, or more frightening.

'I think we should take steps to shut her mouth, permanently,' Sybil went on.

Nausea rose in Zara's throat at the implication in the words.

'*I'm* not going to get done for murder,' she heard Maurice protest. 'Besides, *he* wouldn't like that, he's besotted with her. It would turn him against *us*.'

'He needn't know the truth, stupid! It wouldn't *look* like murder!' Sybil was the strong one in this unholy alliance. 'It should be very easy in a place like this, to arrange an accident.'

Presumably Maurice was looking doubtful, for she snapped at him, 'I tell you, it'd work, and she's daft enough to help us out. She nearly put paid to herself in that thunderstorm . . . pity she didn't. I hope *you* haven't developed a soft spot for the stupid little bitch, though what you could see in her . . .'

'Nothing,' Maurice retorted, 'anyway, *you* did your best to make sure she had no allure for me, didn't you . . . those ridiculous clothes!'

'It was *you* who didn't want her to wear her own. You said familiar things might bring her memory back too quickly.'

Zara knew she'd heard enough. With Tor out for the day, they might never have a better opportunity of putting Sybil's hideous plan into action. She must get away, but how? Tor's car was gone, Maurice kept *his* car locked, the key about his person and now she knew the reason for what had seemed like excessive zeal for her safety. He was frightened, not of her having another accident, but that, once in the car, she might escape him . . . them.

Silently, but swiftly, she tiptoed back to the study. Even now Sybil might have convinced Maurice that he must take action immediately. Even now, he might be coming softly along the passage towards the study. There was no time even for collecting coat and handbag. Any delay could be fatal . . . for her.

Thankful for the jeans and warm sweater borrowed from the unknown's wardrobe, Zara eased open the study window. She slid over the sill, pushed the casement to. There was little cover at the front of the house and she could only hope the two conspirators were still arguing at the rear, as she sped towards the rough lane that led to the farm.

All day a mist had been rising off the moorland, and Zara prayed fervently that, while it would not get too thick, it would be sufficient to hide her from predatory eyes. But, as she hurried along, the mist became denser, making it impossible to see more than a few yards ahead. She must be careful, she thought a trifle hysterically, not to step into a bog, or she would be doing Maurice's evil work for him.

There were no landmarks visible now and it was difficult to determine how much leeway she needed in order to avoid the notorious Wolfstor Mire, to reach Nan's cottage. She stopped fractionally in her stride. Nan Jones, who had a cottage up against the Wolfstor! In her need, her mind had dredged up this memory of a possible sanctuary! But who or what was Nan Jones and why did she remember her existence?

As she stumbled along, she heard a sound, disembodied and eerie, rising in a great swell of hideous noise, engulfing the moorland in its raucous voice. She knew what it was. It was the siren at Princetown, at the prison. One of their convicts had escaped. She shuddered, partly at the thought of the desperation that could urge a man to escape on such a day, and partly with an irrational dread that he might find his way to this part of the moor. Mentally, she shook herself. With the whole of Dartmoor to choose from, why would he come to this one spot? If he had any sense, he would have friends nearby, waiting to get him away, across the Devonshire borders.

Her wanderings had brought her to a stream. She seemed to remember that streams always led somewhere. It was miry at the water's edge, but she hurried along, making what speed she could, through the impenetrable fog. It was raining now, growing dark too and she realised she must have been walking throughout the short winter's afternoon. She was lost. She would never find Nan's cottage now and it would be a miserable, wretched night, unless she could find shelter of some sort. If she didn't fall into a bog, she would probably die of exposure, in which case, she might just as well have stayed where she was and risked meeting her fate at Maurice and Sybil's hands.

At this precise moment of despair, she felt harder ground beneath her feet and she was congratulating herself that it must lead to a proper road, perhaps to some settlement or other, when a great black shape loomed up before her.

For a moment, she believed it to be a distortion of her imagination, a moorland mirage. Then she made contact with what was undoubtedly a warm, living, human being . . . a man . . . and her eyes screwed up in an effort to pierce the miasma that encircled his head and shoulders.

A freak breeze blew aside the mist . . . only for a second, but it was long enough for mind-shattering recognition and Zara began to scream, a cry of horror, of despair, and of unwilling, total recall.

'Well, well,' drawled familiar, hated tones, 'how very convenient. If it isn't my little Zara.'

She shuddered. He had always been fascinated by her petite stature. Large, painfully strong hands gripped her arms.

The wreathing fog swirling around his head gave him the appearance of some evil demon. Mouth sand-dry, her lips unable to form his hated name, she stared up into the well-remembered square face beneath its thatch of cropped fair hair, saw the hardness in the pale blue eyes. Alike, yet so subtly different, a difference emphasised by the lack of a tan, by his

unnatural pallor, a prison pallor ... Michael
Dane, Maurice's twin, and her husband.

No wonder Maurice had meant nothing to her.
Despite the superficial resemblance, Maurice was
a pale shadow compared with the strong,
dominating character of his twin. Maurice was
bad, weak, easily led, Michael was evil, only she
hadn't known that, until it was too late.

'My brother tells me you've forgotten my
existence, Zara. That's very unflattering, something I can't allow.'

Thank goodness Maurice had told Michael of
her amnesia. She could put this knowledge to
good use. How fortunate she hadn't cried out
Michael's name. It would be safer to allow him to
believe her memory was still affected.

'I ... I'm sorry? You must excuse me. You
startled me. I wasn't expecting to meet anyone.
Did you say I know your brother?'

'Don't give me that, Zara!' But his voice held a
shade of doubt. 'My brother is Maurice Dane,
and I'm Michael, remember?'

She remembered only too well, Zara thought
bitterly. It was only incredible to her that she
could have forgotten his existence.

'I do know Maurice, of course. He's my
husband, but I didn't know he had a brother.'
Zara felt quite proud of her ingenuity. Though
the return of her memory had brought with it all
the horror of the past, it had also restored her
natural courage and self-assurance.

'Maurice told you *that*?' He sounded furious,
suspicious. 'What the hell has he been up to?
Have you two been living together as man and
wife?'

'Of course,' Zara said innocently. 'Why shouldn't we?' She knew she was playing with fire, that Michael had a dangerous, almost maniacal temper. But if she could direct it against Maurice instead of against herself . . .

'Why? Why? I'll tell you why, the dirty, double-crossing swine. He should stick to his own wife!'

'But . . . but I'm . . .'

'Oh no you're not, and I'd like to know why he told you you were. *His* wife is called Sybil.'

Zara hadn't needed Michael to tell her that since she remembered now, with frightening clarity, everything that had happened to her, even how she'd first met Sybil and Maurice Dane.

'You're certainly very like Maurice,' she said, feigning surprise. 'But are you *sure* I'm . . .?'

'Who should be sure, if I'm not?' he snapped. 'I'm your husband, Zara, and the sooner you remember it the better. This fellow you're all working for, Maurice didn't mention his name, what's he like?'

'He . . . he's O.K.'

'He'd better be, because you're going to lead me to his place, to the back door, mind, not the front.'

'Why not the front?' she asked. At all costs she must maintain her pose of innocent ignorance. She must gain time, time in which the miraculous might happen, the prison authorities catch up with him.

'Because I've just escaped from Princetown,' he said bluntly, 'and Maurice was supposed to be waiting for me, with a car.' He sounded exasperated. 'Weeks of planning and then the fool didn't turn up. Well, now *you're* going to help me, since my dear brother hasn't kept his side of the bargain.'

That *was* odd, Zara reflected. From the little she'd learned of Maurice Dane before her accident, she knew he had always been totally dominated by his stronger twin.

'You're going to borrow some of your employer's clothes for me, and his car. Then we'll drive away from this benighted place. No one's going to suspect a man and wife on their way home.'

'But,' Zara still played her role, 'I only have your word for it that you *are* my husband.'

His hand took her arm in a crippling vice.

'You'd better believe it! Because although whether you remember or not doesn't matter to me right at this moment, when we're well away, I'll soon *see* that you remember, get me? Right! Lead on!'

'I'm not sure I can find my way.' At least that was the truth. 'I was already lost when I met you.'

'Even so, you'll try. What were you doing out here anyway?'

'I'd been for a walk and got lost,' she improvised.

'In this pea-souper of a fog?' he said scornfully. 'Well, you always were a bit of a fool.'

'Yes,' she muttered, but inaudibly. She must have been a fool, not to have seen through this man, to the brute that strode at her side. Now she knew why her subconscious had so readily rejected the past.

She stumbled on, the escaped convict at her

side. The mist was definitely thinning. Soon there would be no excuse for not leading Michael to Wolfstor.

'Know where you are yet?'

'Yes,' she said reluctantly. The fog was almost gone and she was beginning to recognise landmarks.

'Good! When we get to the house, you can show me where to hole up, while you see if the coast's clear. I could do with some food as well.'

Leaving Michael concealed in a disused outhouse, Zara made her way to the rear entrance. Were Maurice and Sybil still here, she wondered? She had even more reason to fear them, now that she could remember their treatment of her before her accident. She hesitated outside the door, but she was infinitely more afraid of her husband than of his brother, so she went in. There was no one in the kitchen, but an appetising aroma rose from the stove. Sybil had prepared a meal, so she hadn't been expecting to leave Wolfstor immediately. Perhaps they'd intended to hide Michael at the farm, keeping his presence from Tor.

The house was empty, so sign of Maurice, Sybil, *or* of Tor. She hoped that Tor in particular wouldn't return while Michael was here. Agonising fear filled her. Tor and Michael must never meet. She must get her husband away from the farm as quickly as possible.

When Zara had longed so frantically for memory to return, she hadn't dreamt it would be like this, recollection accompanied by shame, unhappiness, but above all else, fear.

The only child of Sir John Sinclair, whose country home was in Gloucestershire, Zara's life had always been one of comfortable affluence, and in addition she had been blessed with a considerable artistic talent. Unlike many girls from wealthy families who could not be bothered to establish themselves in their own right, Zara had been determined to develop her skills. It would never be necessary for her to live off the proceeds of her art, but she burned to prove that she could have done so. She had attended a good art college and it wasn't long before her work had begun to draw attention, appearing in major exhibitions. She received favourable press reviews and before long was receiving as many commissions as she could handle, generally to illustrate factual books, subjects to which her accuracy of line and attention to detail made her work most suited.

'There's someone I'd like you to meet, Zara.' Her agent, Charlie Laing, telephoned her at her London flat, early one Monday morning, a fateful Monday that heralded a whole new dimension to her life. 'A well-known author I have on my books. You may have read him? T. B. Endacott? He's looking for a new illustrator. I've told him you'd be just the ticket. Come round to the office later this morning and I'll introduce you.'

'I don't know.' Zara was doubtful. 'I've quite a few outstanding commissions in hand, as well as another exhibition coming up.'

There's no hurry,' Charlie hastened to assure her, 'he's still doing the groundwork. He travels a lot, but he just happens to be in London this week. I know once you've met him and seen what he has in mind you won't be able to resist, or he you.'

Afterwards, she'd wondered if Charlie had been guilty of deliberate *double entendre*.

Her first thought on seeing Tor Endacott was that she wished she'd paid more attention to her appearance. Instead, following Charlie's call, she had worked flat out until it was time to leave for her appointment, then went as she was, in her normal, workaday jeans and shirt.

Hearing the nature of Tor Endacott's work, the recording of local customs, she'd expected an elderly scholar and the realisation was a complete surprise, a very pleasant surprise. With his height and arresting colouring, he was quite the most attractive man she'd ever met. Nor was there anything of the dry-as-dust scholar about his compelling personality.

'I'm impressed with your style,' he told Zara, as he put down her portfolio, which he had examined carefully.

Zara was surprised. His inscrutable expression had given her the idea that he didn't find her work to his taste.

'But,' the deep, mellow voice went on, 'I'll be frank with you, I'm not sure that Charlie's notion that we should co-operate is such a good one.'

'Fair enough!' Zara was slightly piqued, but it wasn't as if she *needed* any more work at present. She rose to leave.

'Now hold on!' Charlie interposed. 'Don't make any hasty decisions. You might both regret it later on.'

'Charlie!' Tor Endacott got his word in first, before Zara could retort. 'You know my views about working with women. Now old Fred Linklater was ideal. He . . .'

'But Fred Linklater is dead,' Charlie said bluntly, 'and be honest, Endacott, his style was a bit dated. Now Zara here has a nice fresh technique . . .'

'And Zara,' she interrupted, chin proudly tip-tilted, 'also has plenty of commissions. I'm not pushing myself on to someone who doesn't want me. Forget it, Charlie!'

'No!' her agent said stubbornly. 'I'm *not* going to forget it, and I'm not going to let you two throw away a chance like this, one which could benefit *both* of you.'

'And which would, incidentally, benefit *you*, Charlie,' Tor put in, a wry smile making his attractive features even more so.

'And you can't *make* two people work together,' Zara pointed out.

'True, but I can *suggest* that you give the idea a bit more thought, talk it over. Why don't we all have lunch together?'

'Oh, but . . .' Taken aback, Zara would have protested further but for Tor Endacott's intervention.

'All right, Charlie, we'll *talk*, but only because I think Miss Sinclair's due an explanation. She's wasted good working time coming here.'

'Thank you,' Zara interrupted, 'but I've no intention of wasting any more.'

'You do *eat* occasionally, I suppose?'

'Of course, but . . .'

'Then may I point out that it *is* lunchtime. I assume you don't work through your break.'

'Sometimes. I often forget time when I'm busy.'

'So do I.' Suddenly his face broke into its oddly disarming smile. 'Come, Miss Sinclair, have lunch with me. Let me excuse my apparent boorishness. My reluctance to work with you isn't personal, you know. I do have very good reasons.'

Only a moment ago determined to dislike this man, Zara found herself, unaccountably, hesitating. There was something very winning about that smile, the tone in which his invitation had been repeated.

'Miss Sinclair?'

'Oh, all right,' she capitulated and she thought she saw an expression of unwilling admiration in his strange green eyes, as she added defiantly, 'But don't get the wrong idea. I'm not lunching with you because I hope you'll change your mind. I'm coming, because it *is* lunchtime and I'm hungry.'

'So am I!' Charlie Laing rose with alacrity from behind his desk.

'Sorry, Charlie!' Tor Endacott shook his head. 'As this won't be a business lunch, agents aren't invited. This is just between me and Miss Sinclair.'

Zara had difficulty in hiding a smile. Plump little Charlie liked nothing better than a leisurely business lunch, the food giving him as much if not more satisfaction than making a good deal. Uncharacteristically, however, Charlie did not press the point, but sank back into his chair with only a rueful shrug.

Wondering at this, Zara looked back over her shoulder as they left, intending to give him a wry smile of commiseration and surprising instead a conspiratorial wink-cum-grimace distorting her agent's face. What was the wily Charlie up to now?

Considering the inauspicious start to their acquaintance, Zara found herself liking the attractive author. Over lunch he made no reference to the contentious subject of their proposed collaboration, but talked interestingly and knowledgeably on a wide variety of subjects, and Zara listened with unfeigned interest as he told her of his beginnings as the son of a small West Country Farmer. He'd been a scholarship boy and he'd worked hard. Zara was glad she could tell him in return how, despite her greater advantages, she had shared his determination to succeed in her own right, on her own merits.

'At one point, I decided to work my way round the world,' Tor told his absorbed hearer. 'I rubbed shoulders with all sorts. But best of all, I learnt a lot about the folklore of the countries I worked in, and that set the foundation of my interest. I'd always been an avid reader and I'd always been convinced I could write. Now I knew what about.'

Zara found him utterly fascinating, not just for his appearance, though she was very aware that he held a strong attraction for her, but also because their minds seemed to be in such total accord. Charlie had been right. Here was a man with whom and for whom she would be more than happy to work, and but for *his* unwillingness, might well have done so.

The meal was over, their table already in demand by other diners and still Tor Endacott had not touched on the real reason for their lunching together.

'Do you really have to work this afternoon?' he asked her suddenly. 'The weather's so good, it seems a crime to spend it cooped up in an office.'

'I don't have an office,' she told him, 'I work from home, my flat.' It was true she didn't feel like working, although, when she'd left her current project, she had been eager to return to it. Now she felt vaguely unsettled and she was realistic enough to admit to herself that her reluctance stemmed from her enjoyment of Tor Endacott's company and the wish that their acquaintance need not be so short-lived.

Thus, after a token show of reluctance, she allowed herself to be persuaded to take a walk through Hyde Park with him. Instead of talking about himself, as he had over lunch, he proceeded to draw Zara out, eliciting more details of her work and her life, past and present.

'And are *you* totally dedicated to your career? Or is there a man in your life somewhere? What about the future?'

'If by dedication you mean having no time for a social life, no, I can't claim to be "dedicated". As to the future,' she shrugged, 'I'd like to get married some day, I suppose, but I'm in no hurry and I'd hope . . . no . . . I *mean* to go on working. My art means far too much to me to ever give it up.'

'So there's no current boyfriend to monitor your activities?'

'No.' Zara smiled wryly. 'Only an ex-one, who won't take no for an answer. He keeps writing and phoning.'

'But he's out of luck?'

'Yes. Michael's good company, but he's not good husband material.'

'Neither am I,' Tor said shortly, and, as she looked at him in surprise, 'he had to get around to the subject eventually, though I admit I've been putting it off.'

'Why should we have to discuss your potential, or lack of it, as a husband?' Zara asked, bewildered.

'It's not *that* exactly, just part of why I don't care to have a woman working with me. Women tend to get emotionally involved, to get possessive. I've had the experience twice of little fools making me a target for their romantic fantasising. That's why I'm sorry to lose old Fred. I need an artist, but I don't need a bed-warmer. I'm a traveller by nature. I don't want to be tied down.'

Zara felt herself bristling. The arrogant conceit of the man. Did he really expect *every* woman to be like that, to fall head over heels in love with him?

'Well, you wouldn't have had to worry about *that* in *my* case,' she told him somewhat tartly.

'Oh?' The green eyes surveyed her speculatively. 'How so?'

'For one thing, I'm not the type that "moons" or "fantasises", just because my colleague happens to be a *man*. You'd have to have an awful lot going for you besides *that*.'

'Really?' he said thoughtfully. 'You *do* reassure me.'

'Not that there's any need,' she pointed out, 'since we *won't be* collaborating.'

'No. No, although ... if I weren't so busy, it could be very interesting to find out just what qualities *would* turn you on.'

'As you don't have them,' she riposted, 'you wouldn't find out anyway.' Zara was, she discovered, enjoying this slightly hostile and yet almost flirtatious repartee. It was a pity in a way, she thought, that she would have no opportunity to demonstrate that she *was* first and foremost a professional artist, and not the husband-hunter he seemed to think all women were by nature.

'It's getting late,' Tor said almost abruptly. 'Since I've already "wasted" most of your day, I suppose you wouldn't care to spend the rest of it with me? Have dinner? At my place?'

Carefully, Zara hid the sudden amusement she felt. Tor hadn't been quite able to conceal the pique her denial of his appeal had caused him. She felt a little frisson of excitement at the thought that he might intend to challenge her avowed immunity to him.

'Why not?' she said lightly. 'It's too late to start work now.' In actual fact, Zara very often worked on into the evening and late at night, but she found herself glad of this excuse not to part from Tor just yet.

She had expected that he would have dinner sent in from a nearby restaurant, but when he took her back to his apartment, she found that his roving life had also made him totally independent. In his small kitchenette they worked together harmoniously, grilling steaks, which they ate with salad, finishing their meal with fresh fruit.

'I expect you're used to far more sophisticated fare,' Tor said ruefully. 'But I live alone, can't bear servants messing around me, so I've learnt to eat with the minimum of fuss. It leaves me more time for my work.'

Zara was able to assure him, truthfully, that she did the same.

'But you're a better cook than I am!' she admitted.

Over coffee, she found herself taking every opportunity for surreptitious scrutiny of him and she was honest enough with herself to admit that, despite her disclaimer, she found him very attractive, and that she wished he did want her to work with him. If they had collaborated, was it possible theirs could have progressed beyond a purely business relationship? Even so, she flushed, when she found herself picturing how well his tall, muscular body would strip, and unexpectedly meeting his gaze, she lowered her own eyes, in the sudden fear that he might be able to read her thoughts.

She was half disappointed, half relieved, when, after their meal, the conversation remained on a purely matter-of-fact level, with no personalities or innuendoes intruding. Perhaps, she thought with amused chagrin, *he* didn't find *her* at all attractive. He insisted on escorting her back to her flat, but he didn't suggest that she invite him in and Zara felt a sharp pang of regret as he turned to leave. Then, just as she inserted the key in her front door, he swung back.

'Of course,' he said brusquely, 'just because we're not going to work together, doesn't mean we can't be . . . friends?'

'I suppose not,' she said cautiously, after a few deliberate seconds of reflection. He mustn't see how her heart had lifted joyously at this reprieve.

Suddenly, his smile lit up his face.

'Good. Then I'll ring you . . . tomorrow?'

They met several times in the next few days and it did occur to Zara to wonder what had happened to the extensive research Tor was supposed to be undertaking, for he seemed in no hurry to get back to his work. Though his manner was still one of easy camaraderie, Zara could not dispel the notion that Tor was, perhaps unwillingly, attracted physically to her. There was the occasional hint of it in his manner towards her as he guided her through doorways, assisted her in and out of taxis. It was when they danced that she was nearly positive. Surely it wasn't only her body that was intimately aware of the sensuous warmth that seemed to flow between them? Not only her body that reacted to every little accidental movement that made contact between them? Sometimes she was not even sure if these incidents were in fact accidental. But though she waited, his declaration never came.

CHAPTER FIVE

THOUGH surprised by Tor's request that she do so, Zara took him to her Gloucestershire home one weekend, pleased to find that her father too liked the personable author. She had always found it a good test of any friend, to see them against her home background and particularly in company with her father.

'A vast improvement over the young men you've brought home in the past and certainly over the last one, that Michael fellow you brought here once or twice last year,' Sir John commented. 'You in love with this one, by any chance?'

'N ... no ... of course not,' Zara denied hastily. But was she? She hoped not, because it would make their eventual parting much harder and recently Tor had begun to talk of the necessity of his getting back to work.

'I'm in the midst of researching Devonshire folk lore,' he told her one day. 'Heaven only knows why I haven't done it before. It's been on my doorstep all my life.' Then, to her astonishment he added, albeit abruptly, 'And I've changed my mind. I *would* like you to work with me on this book ... that's if you're still interested, of course?' His tone made it uncertain whether he hoped she would accept or refuse.

'Well, that's unexpected,' Zara said, unable to prevent the edge of sarcasm to her voice. 'You're not afraid I might "complicate" your life?'

'No.' He hesitated, then: 'I've come to the conclusion that you're sensible and mature enough to handle a business relationship without emotional complications arising.' He sounded almost pompous, quite unlike his natural self.

'*Have you?*' Zara asked tautly. 'So *you've* changed your mind! But suppose I haven't? You haven't asked me if I *want* to collaborate with you.'

'Zara?' Dark eyebrows shot up in enquiry, 'What's wrong? What have I said? I thought we were friends? My words were *meant* to be complimentary.'

'Oh, was *that* what you meant?' Zara's tone, though ironic, was quiet. She didn't feel at all complimented by Tor's assurance that she wouldn't upset the even tenor of his working life.

'What I'd like,' he continued, without, apparently, being aware that she was still annoyed, 'is for you to come down to Wolfstor Farm with me. It would give you a chance to absorb the atmosphere of the area.'

'How long would you expect me to stay?' Pique notwithstanding, his invitation excited Zara with the possibilities it offered, but it frightened her too. She felt shaken by the intensity of the instincts that urged her to accept this opportunity to spend more time in Tor's company ... and quite alone, since he had no use for servants.

'I had thought a month? It may not appeal to you, of course,' he went on hastily, 'it's completely isolated, no social life. It'd be just us ... and the moor.' It wasn't his words so much as his tone that made her tremble at the pictures he drew for her ... seclusion, an inevitably greater intimacy? His description of his lonely home held no fears for her. By now she knew she would have gone with him anywhere and she knew why. Many men had claimed to be in love with Zara, but for the first time in her life, *she* was in love . . . but her love was unlikely to be returned. Was it wise to take the risk of being badly hurt?

Zara loved Wolfstor Farm, as she had been sure she would. She knew she would be more than content to live there forever, with Tor, if only he would suggest it. For the month's stay, she had brought with her a large part of her wardrobe. It gave her presence at Wolfstor a warm feeling of permanence, to see her own clothes hanging in the spare bedroom.

The first few days at the farm were spent by Zara looking through Tor's earlier books, to get some idea of the type of illustration that would be expected of her, Tor expounding his ideas for his new book, asking her opinion as to the best way of portraying the various legends and items of folklore. But busy as they were, Zara was not too engrossed in her work to be unaware of Tor's magnetically virile attraction for her.

She couldn't help wondering what it would be like if he were interested in her. The subject had never arisen again, but it didn't appear to Zara that he had ever been married and he must be thirty-five or thereabouts. Had there been *any* women in Tor's life? Surely there must have been. In spite of his dedication to his work, he was only human. Had he ever asked any other woman to stay at Wolfstor, ever made love to any of them? She wished she knew, then, contrarily, was glad she didn't. The thought of Tor making

Yes, become a Harlequin home subscriber and the celebration goes on forever.

To begin with we'll send you:

- **4 new Harlequin Presents novels — Free**
- **an elegant, purse-size manicure set — Free**
- **and an exciting mystery bonus — Free**

And that's not all! Special extras — Three more reasons to celebrate

4. Money-Saving Home Delivery That's right! When you become a Harlequin home subscriber the excitement, romance and far-away adventures of Harlequin Presents novels can be yours for previewing in the convenience of your own home **at less than retail prices.** Here's how it works. Every month we'll deliver eight new books right to your door. If you decide to keep them, they'll be yours for only $1.75! That's 20¢ less per book than what you pay in stores. And there is **no charge for shipping and handling.**

5. Free Monthly Newsletter — It's "Heart to Heart" — the indispensable insider's look at our most popular writers and their up-coming novels. Now you can have a behind-the-scenes look at the fascinating world of Harlequin! It's an added bonus you'll look forward to every month!

6. More Surprise Gifts — Because our home subscribers are our most valued readers, we'll be sending you additional free gifts from time to time — as a token of our appreciation.

This beautiful manicure set will be a useful and elegant item to carry in your handbag. Its rich burgundy case is a perfect expression of your style and good taste. And it's yours free in this amazing Harlequin celebration!

HARLEQUIN READER SERVICE
FREE OFFER CARD

4 FREE BOOKS

ELEGANT MANICURE SET – FREE

FREE MYSTERY BONUS

PLACE YOUR BALLOON STICKER HERE!

MONEY SAVING HOME DELIVERY

FREE FACT-FILLED NEWSLETTER

MORE SURPRISE GIFTS THROUGHOUT THE YEAR – FREE

☐ **YES!** Please send me my four Harlequin Presents novels **Free,** along with my manicure set and my **free mystery gift.** Then send me eight new Harlequin Presents novels every month and bill me just $1.75 per book (20¢ less than retail), with no extra charges for shipping and handling. If I am not completely satisfied, I may return a shipment and cancel at any time. **The free books, manicure set and mystery gift remain mine to keep.**

108 CIP CAKK

FIRST NAME _____ LAST NAME _____
            (PLEASE PRINT)

ADDRESS _____ APT. _____

CITY _____ PROV./STATE _____

POSTAL CODE / ZIP _____

Remember! To receive your four free books, manicure set and surprise mystery bonus return the postpaid card below. But don't delay!

DETACH & MAIL CARD TODAY

If card has been removed, write to: Harlequin Reader Service, 901 Fuhrmann Blvd., P.O. Box 1394, Buffalo, NY 14240-9963

love to other women awoke a stinging jealousy
within her that amounted to physical pain.

However, despite their long hours in Tor's
study, ostensibly the purpose of her visit was that
she might absorb the atmosphere of the
Devonshire countryside and this she certainly
did, as Tor drove them from site to site in his
comically small car. Some days, they rode out on
small, sturdy ponies, native to Dartmoor. They
visited one or two of the little villages edging the
moor, stopping occasionally where there was a
particularly appealing legend to relate, and Zara
made a few preliminary sketches.

'I'm looking forward to our co-operation on this
book,' Tor told her as, one evening, they pored
over the results of their day's outing. 'I think
your drawings are going to lift it into a class of its
own, a classic of its kind.' He went to the shelves
which held his previous books and selected a
volume, opening it at one of the illustrations.
'This chap was good, but not a patch on you.
Your work has an indescribable quality, which
enhances the legends.'

A particularly productive day was that on
which they paid a visit to a friend of Tor's who
was, Zara gathered from his description, something of a local character. They rode out over the
dark brown, undulating heath, skirting the
perilous Wolfstor Mire, making towards the
frowning granite crest of the Wolfstor itself. It
loomed gloomy and sullen-looking, even on this
pleasant summer's day. Yet, despite its foreboding
presence, something about it was powerfully
attractive to the imaginative girl.

'Watch out for boggy places,' Tor told her, as

they rode, 'even on what may *look* like safe ground.'

As they rode, she studied him. His ascetic profile showed a strong pleasure in his surroundings. Though he was a good mixer when in company, and widely travelled, she felt he was basically a reserved man, as witness his desire for this solitude, his secluded home. Was he the kind of man who would *ever* wish to share his life with a woman, to seek a permanent relationship?

As they drew nearer to the tor, she could see, standing almost against its side, a rough granite dwelling.

'That's where your friend lives?' Zara asked incredulously. It was no beauty spot, too near to the quaking Wolfstor mire for comfort, a fearsome, lonely spot.

But the greystone cottage was sturdily built, its walls thick, its roof of thatch. The ancient stones were grown about with lichens and mosses, a natural camouflage making it almost indistinguishable from the tor against whose strong outline it stood.

Sturdy, diminutive and brown skinned, Tor's friend, Nan Jones, seemed a part of her wild surroundings, complexion and white hair the products of some sixty or so years of Dartmoor weather. She treated Tor with a curious mixture of respect and scolding affection.

'Why haven't ee been to see I these many weeks?' she demanded, then, 'No, don't ee be telling me. I have eyes. I can see,' and she subjected Zara to an interested appraisal, which, though thorough, was not in the least impertinent. At last she nodded, as though satisfied. 'This one'll do, Tor lad. I can tell. Old Nan knows, don't she though?'

There *was* something strangely compelling about the old woman's dark, penetrating eyes, which gave Zara the feeling that Nan did know things unrevealed to others. Meeting Tor's gaze, she found it unusually intent upon her, almost, she thought fancifully, as if he were thinking over Nan's recommendation, trying to see Zara with the old woman's eyes. Zara flushed self-consciously and looked away, relieved when Nan drew Tor's attention back to herself.

'Writing more of your learned books, are ee?' the old woman asked, as she pressed glasses of home-made wine upon them. 'And whose secrets be ee diggin' out now?'

'Yours, I hope, Nan,' Tor said gravely. 'I've wandered all over this country of ours, collecting all kinds of legends and it suddenly occurred to me that I'd been neglecting my own back yard.'

The old woman needed little coaxing to talk, the stories pouring from her in a vast stream, fact mingled with legend, history with myth and superstition. Not only that, but, as the afternoon progressed, Zara came to the conclusion that, years ago, Nan Jones would have been regarded as a witch, for her forays on to the moor to gather herbs and berries, her understanding of the medical qualities of different plants. Tor echoed Zara's thoughts, saying affectionately:

'You're an old witch, Nan, that's what you are.'

Quite unruffled, the old lady admitted the truth of his statement, with as much pride as if he had offered her the rarest compliment.

'That I be, but at least I be a white witch. Folks round here reckon my magic does 'em nothing but good.'

'Nan tells fortunes too,' Tor told Zara. 'Let her read *your* hand.'

'Oh . . . I don't think . . . I don't believe in . . .'

But before she could protest further, Nan took possession of her hands, turning them palms uppermost. Keen eyes, undimmed by age, scanned the smooth flesh.

'Talented hands, artistic hands . . .' Then the old lady's face screwed up into puzzled lines. 'Your future is strangely clouded, m'dear. 'Tis like the mist that times veils the moor. I can see a man though . . . tall, fair-haired!' She paused to look at Tor, at his dark auburn waves. 'There's not one, but two men in your life, m'dear. Very similar types they be and they'll have you fair mazed between them.'

This was all nonsense, of course, Zara told herself. The only fair-headed man in her life had been Michael Dane, a fellow art student whom she had dated several times and who was still persistent in his attempts to renew a friendship which had ended a short while before she'd met Tor. Nan's voice rose in a sudden harsh crescendo.

'You mustn't trust 'em! No, don't you trust 'em, girl! I see evil . . . death . . . murder . . . and I see the mire, Wolfstor Mire, the end of it all.' Urgently, she gripped Zara's hands. 'Stay you away from the mire, child, stay away from those men.'

Zara must have paled, for suddenly Tor intervened.

'Enough, Nan, you're scaring the girl out of her wits.'

Reluctantly, Nan released the trembling hands. 'Afearing her I may be,' she muttered stubbornly, 'but 'tis true every word and forewarned is forearmed.'

Zara was unutterably relieved when Tor said they must leave. Though she wasn't superstitious, the old woman's words had shaken her considerably. She followed him outside, promising, untruthfully, that she would visit Nan again. But she couldn't escape the parting words flung after her, as they rode away.

'I be bound to tell what I see, and I see death in your hand, death on Dartmoor.'

'*Did* Nan frighten you?' Tor asked, as they rode away from the cottage.

'N . . . no, at least . . . *you* don't think she can really foresee the future?'

'Of course not,' Tor said briskly, perhaps a little too briskly, Zara wondered. 'But at least remember *one* of her warnings, stay away from the mire!'

'And that's just common sense,' Zara agreed. She laughed, shaking off the cloud that, briefly, had settled over her. 'It doesn't need clairvoyance to tell anyone *that*.' She urged her pony forward a little. On the well-worn sheep tracks that crossed the moorland it was best to ride single file. As she did so, a bird rose from cover, right beneath her pony's feet and the normally stolid little animal behaved with uncharacteristic skittishness, rearing up, then starting forward, taking Zara unawares.

Though Sir John Sinclair was a keen horseman

and rider to hounds, Zara had never shared her father's interest, and though she had by now become accustomed to the moorland pony's gait, she was not a sufficiently accomplished rider to check his headlong flight.

Before long, her mount was going at a good gallop. Travelling at an amazing speed, considering his low stature, her pony suddenly plunged into a soft place and taken by surprise, Zara was sent flying over his head. Then the pony was half way up his sides in the mire and beating wildly with his forelegs. Zara herself had been fortunate enough to land on comparatively firm ground. As she struggled to her feet, dimly aware of the painful bruises that would follow her encounter with the earth, Tor was already going to the pony's rescue. Had he no concern for *her*? Then reason asserted itself. A swift glance would have assured him that she was relatively unharmed, whereas her mount was in imminent danger. Banishing her momentary pique, she ran to Tor's assistance. Together, taking hold of the reins, they pulled the pony towards them, until he was able to set his forelegs upon harder ground. Then, struggling vigorously, he pulled himself out, covered with mud and trembling violently.

With the pony safe, to Zara's dismay, shock set in and she began to shake almost as badly as the animal, her lips quivering. Tor took one look at her, dropped the pony's reins, and pulled her into his arms.

'It's all right, my darling. It's all right. You're safe, thank God.'

Had he *meant* that endearment? Had he even noticed that he'd used it?

'It . . . it was just *that* happening, so soon after Nan's prediction,' Zara said and essayed a laugh, a faint failure.

'Pure coincidence!' he said the words almost fiercely, but his arms tightened around her and Zara's tremors increased, but caused now by sensations far removed from shock and fear. Waves of sheer eroticism flowed through her at Tor's nearness and without conscious volition, she found herself clinging to him.

'Zara?' He said her name almost wonderingly, bringing her to a shamed realisation of her behaviour. Immediately she tried to move away.

'I . . . I'm sorry. It . . . it was just the fright. I'm all right now . . . truly.'

But he didn't release her. Instead, one hand captured her chin, searching eyes scanned the pale oval of her face.

'Zara?' There was a sense of greater urgency in his questioning, but she tried to evade its implications.

'I . . . I don't usually go to pieces so easily.' She fought to avoid the penetrating green gaze that seemed as if it would read every tumultuous thought in her reeling brain.

'No,' he agreed almost sombrely, and his thumb moved caressingly across the full curve of her tremulous lips. 'And neither do I, but when I saw you fall . . . thought for one hideous moment how you could have . . .' He jerked her suddenly closer. 'You gave me one hell of a fright.' His hands were moving caressingly on her hips. 'It made me realise just how much . . . I can think of a good remedy for shock,' he went on huskily, 'for both of us.'

She looked up at him questioningly, unwarily, and seeing the twisted expression of his features, she could not doubt his sincerity, when he claimed to have been concerned for her. But he spent no more time in words, bending to possess her willing mouth.

'Zara, oh Zara.' At last he freed his lips long enough to say her name, on a note of ragged urgency.

She clung to him in feverish arousal, all the pent-up longing of the past weeks released, his searing passion making her arch against him with a desperate need.

'Let's go home!' He whispered the words into the ear his teeth were tormenting. 'I can't make love to you here.' He held her face between his hands, watching her expression, waiting for her reply. 'And I *want* to make love to you.'

'You ... you want to ... to ...' she said haltingly. 'But ...'

'Can you doubt it?' and she couldn't, when every tautened muscle of his body was reinforcing the words he spoke.

He urged her to walk on then, and in a dream she moved beside him, his arm tightly about her shoulders, the docile ponies following. Let's go home, he'd said, as if he looked upon the farm as her home too. Did he? Wonderingly, she looked up at him and with a sound like a groan, he bent to kiss her once more.

'Dear God! Zara! Don't look at me like that, or I *shall* make love to you here and now and I don't want that. I want to make love to you in comfort, slowly and carefully. I want to know and explore every inch of you, with my lips, my hands ...'

She felt herself beginning to shake again, uncontrollably, with the fierceness of her own desire. But she mustn't give in to it, to him, so easily, so wantonly. She loved him, but he had spoken no word of love, only of desire.

'No, Tor, please . . . let me go.' She struggled.

'You don't mean that, Zara. Stop fighting me. Do you think I haven't been aware, all along, of this sexual attraction between us, that I haven't fought against it . . .'

'No . . .'

'Zara,' his voice was warmly amused, 'don't keep saying no, when *you* know and *I* know that you mean yes.'

Again he moved on and bemusedly, she went with him, in her dreamlike state scarcely aware of her surroundings, until the ponies' hoofs clattered on the cobbled courtyard. She was tensely aware of Tor's nearness, of his pent-up eagerness, as they worked side by side rubbing down the ponies, knew that he was as aware of her, but too conscientious a countryman to neglect his animals. But at last, when the grooming was finished, he took both her hands in his.

'And now, Zara, we have time, all the time in the world, to talk . . . and to make love,' he told her softly. 'But first, I think, a bath, don't you? We both have a distinct aura of saddle-soap and horseflesh, not to mention a liberal coating of mud.'

It was a reprieve from decision and Zara lingered in the bath, wallowing in scented oils and soaps, shampooing her dark curls, which had not escaped the mire. She knew she was deliberately postponing the inevitable confrontation

with Tor, the moment of decision, of truth. A
sensuous quiver, half fear, half longing ran
through her and she turned on the hot tap once
more, in an effort to dispel the little shivers that
ran along her spine.

A knock on the bathroom door sounded above
the running water. She made no reply, but
tension knotted her stomach, a tension that
relaxed as she recalled the heavy old-fashioned
bolt on the door . . . which she *hadn't* secured. In a
hurry to soak the mud from her person, she
realised she'd forgotten. Motionless she watched
the door open, saw Tor, clad only in a short silk
dressing gown that clung revealingly to his
muscular frame, that fell open at the knee to
display muscular thighs with the soft sheen of
auburn hairs.

'G . . . go away,' she hissed, looking vainly for
something with which to cover herself.

'You don't mean that.' His eyes seemed to sear
a molten trail over her body, as he assessed
everything that the rapidly dispersing bubbles
were leaving open to his inspection. 'Let me help
you.' He had taken a large, fluffy towel from the
airing cupboard and now he stood over her,
holding it out invitingly. It was tempting to go
into that proffered embrace, but . . .

'I'm not getting out of this bath till you go.'

'I know who'll enjoy the waiting most,' he
murmured, 'and that water must be getting
awfully cold.'

Defiantly, she reached for the hot tap, but he
restrained her.

'What an extravagant woman you are. I'm
afraid I can't let you use any more hot water.'

'Please . . . I . . .'

'I'm waiting, Zara,' he said inexorably.

Shaking, though she couldn't be sure whether it was from the cooling water, or from nerves, Zara stood, turning her back upon him, reaching behind her for the only security offered to her, the towel. But he evaded her seeking fingers, and wrapped it about her himself, his arms closing round her like a vice, trapping her in the soft folds, lifting her out on to the carpeted floor. Then, by superior strength, easily overcoming her resistance, he turned her to face him.

'There now, that wasn't so bad, was it?' he enquired murmurously.

'I . . .' Bemused blue-grey eyes could not evade the hypnotic enslavement of his and she knew, even before his auburn head bent towards her, that she couldn't, didn't *want* to resist him.

He kissed her, long and searchingly, their bodies coming together with a need that seemed to ignite spontaneously between them. Then his eyes held hers once more, in a long intent stare, an unmistakable question in his.

'Zara, you know this isn't enough, can never be enough, for me, for us? Is it the same for you? Tell me it is.' And as she whispered a tremulous affirmation, his mouth returned to hers.

She slid her hands inside his robe, her fingertips exploring, memorising the muscular contours of his back, his chest, his heart thudding beneath her fingers. Her breath caught on a little hiss of satisfaction as she felt the aroused tension of him, felt his hands tracing the outline of her body, pressing her to his.

'Has there ever been . . . anyone else?' Tor

asked huskily and a satisfied groan reverberated in his throat as she told him there never had been.

'Not like this,' she whispered, 'and there never will be.' She was glad, Zara thought, that she never had given herself to anyone else, for she had no doubt now that she *would* give herself to Tor and find no wrong in doing so, because she loved him.

'And you'll let *me* love you?' It was part question, part assertion. He must know from her responses how much she wanted him.

Wordlessly, she nodded, her throat tight with emotion, delicious tremors shivering through her body at the thought of what was about to happen to her . . . to them.

His hands shaped the hardened swell of her breasts, the arousal of their central peaks, and weakness assailed her legs as she ached with her need of him. It was exciting, yet terrifying too, this realisation that, in the whole world, only Tor had the key to such happiness. If she should ever lose him after this . . .

'Tor?' she whispered. 'You *do* love *me*? You . . .'

'Never doubt it,' he murmured into the blue-black cloud of her hair. It was impossible for him to disguise his need of her and Zara swallowed, as he went on, 'And now I'm going to show you just how much.'

He swung her up into his arms, carried her into his room, set her down on his bed. His lips, his hands were demanding, arousing sensations of internal explosion, leaving her drained, yet stirring every nerve she possessed.

'You're not afraid?'

'No ... oh no!' How could she be afraid of Tor?

Swiftly, he undressed, so that they lay; warm, passion-filled bodies against each other, no obstacles between them. His kisses were becoming more intimate, her body seemed to tingle where it touched his. She knew there was no going back, even if she had wanted to retreat and she moved under him, with a wantonness she hadn't known herself capable of, her low, insistent moan an unmistakable invitation to his possession.

His fingers plunged deeply into her hair, his lips burnt a fiery trail between her breasts, down over the silky smoothness of her stomach, until his hands slid beneath her thighs.

'Zara,' he paused in his exploration, 'I'll try not to hurt you. The first time can be ...'

'I know,' she whispered, 'and I'm not afraid, not with you. I want you, Tor.'

He moved against and into her and any slight sensation of pain was lost in the joyous surge of pleasure they shared, as incoherent words of love and satisfaction spilled from their seeking lips.

In the final week of her stay at Wolfstor Farm, Zara seemed to exist in an idyll of perfect happiness, every waking and every sleeping moment spent in Tor's company. She felt she could ask nothing more of life than this, to fall asleep in his arms and to wake each morning to find him beside her, eager and ready to make love to her again.

It was with reluctance that they left the farmhouse to return to London, but both had outstanding commitments, too long neglected. In Zara's case it was drawings for other clients, in Tor's a book on Scottish legends to be completed, for which purpose he must return to Scotland for a few days.

London seemed airless and overcrowded after the peace and solitude of the moors and as they paid off the taxi which had brought them from the station to Zara's flat, she mentioned this to Tor.

'I always thought I liked being a city-dweller, but now I'm not so sure. I . . . I think I've fallen in love with your Dartmoor.'

'Only with Dartmoor?' he teased, bending over her, unashamedly kissing her in front of interested passers-by. 'Then don't worry, darling, we'll be going back quite soon, once we've sorted out our respective affairs. I imagine you'll be able to work from Wolfstor as easily as from here?'

Her blue-grey eyes twinkled mischievously, as she returned his ardent gaze.

'Maybe,' her tone became demure, 'if there aren't too many . . . "distractions".'

'I don't think I can guarantee that,' he murmured, his voice suddenly husky. Then, with an urgency that excited her, 'Zara, it seems such a long time since I made love to you.'

She glanced at her watch.

'Oh, it is,' she agreed, still demure, 'all of eight hours ago.'

'Then what are we waiting for?' He urged her towards the entrance of her apartment block and with her heart beating rapidly at his never-failing effect upon her, Zara was as eager as he to reach her flat.

But their way was unexpectedly blocked by one

of the onlookers, a tall, fair-haired man, whose face and voice reproached Zara as his blue eyes missed no detail of Tor's appearance, his possessive manner.

'I've called every day for the last month, Zara. I've even been in touch with your father, but nobody seemed to know where you were.'

Despite Tor's hand, still urgent at her elbow, Zara paused, albeit reluctantly. Michael Dane was an old if a former friend and she couldn't treat him discourteously, even though she wished he were not so assiduous in his continued pursuit of her.

'Hallo, Michael. Yes, I've been away, on a business trip.'

'Oh?' His gaze went enquiringly from her to Tor, to the other man's impatient attentiveness.

'Zara,' Tor interrupted, 'if you'll give me your keys, I'll wait for you upstairs. O.K. if I take a shower?' and, as she nodded, excitement thrilling through her as she knew he wanted her to join him in that shower, 'Don't be long . . . darling.'

With Tor's disappearance, she turned back to Michael, her anxiety to join her lover making her voice a little sharp.

'Michael, why do you keep coming round here? I did tell you it was all over between us. You're wasting your time.'

'I don't think so.' His voice was mild, but there was suppressed anger in the blue eyes. '*I'm* still in love with *you*. I still want to marry you and I'm jealous of every other man you spend any time with. Who *is* this fellow?' He jerked his head towards the apartment block. 'You seem to allow him a lot of familiarity.'

'Just an author I'm collaborating with.' She didn't want to discuss Tor with Michael. She was exasperated, not only by his persistence, but because her whole being was crying out to be in Tor's arms once more. Right now he was waiting for her, his bronzed muscular limbs glistening under the tingling shower. 'Our friendship ended a long time ago, Michael. You've no *right* to be jealous of anyone I see. I'm sorry, but I must go in now.'

'To *him*?'

'That's *my* business.' Then her tone softened a little. 'Look, Mike, I'm ... I'm very flattered that you're still fond of me. I'd hoped that we'd parted as friends ...'

'I can never think of you as just a friend.' His words came jerkily, intensely. 'I haven't given up yet, Zara. You'll come to your senses one day and I'll be waiting for you.'

'Michael ...'

'No, don't say any more, Zara. Don't burn your bridges. I shan't. I won't give up hoping until I see you coming out of church on someone else's arm.' For a moment, his hand gripped her shoulder and she could have sworn there was an emotional brilliance in the blue eyes. 'I *want* you, Zara!'

Murmuring something incoherent, she pulled herself free and ran inside the building, turning, despite herself, on the threshold, to see Michael Dane still standing where she'd left him, the same intense expression of determination on his face. But as she ran upstairs to her apartment, the image of Michael began to fade, replaced by that of Tor as he waited eagerly for her. So Michael had sworn he wouldn't give up until he saw her married? Well, that event wasn't too far distant. With this exultant thought she ran into Tor's open arms.

The thought, tinged with satisfaction, with awe, touched the periphery of her brain once more a while later, as she lay, passion-spent in his arms.

'When we're married it will be like this always.' She hardly realised she had spoken the words aloud, until she felt Tor tense.

'Good Lord, what's all this about marriage?'

Zara froze. She couldn't have understood him correctly.

'You . . .' she began, but he was shaking his auburn head firmly.

'Sorry, love, but I haven't mentioned marriage, deliberately. You *know* my feelings about being tied. I thought it was understood . . .'

Zara choked on an angry sob, as she struggled to escape his muscular arms.

'L . . . let me go . . . you . . . you . . .'

'Now, now,' he chided, half teasingly, 'there's no need for all that. You're an adult woman. I assumed . . . or you gave me to understand . . . that you felt the same way. For a career woman, it's no bad thing to have a relationship without strings. It can be just as enduring as marriage . . . even more so in some cases. Just look at the number of celebrities who . . .'

'Stop it! Stop it! Don't say another word.' Zara was not to be consoled by such tenets. She was no prude, or she would never have given herself to Tor so freely, and indeed she knew now just how passionate *was* her nature, but she *was* conventional to a certain extent, had genuinely believed she had overcome Tor's inhibitions regarding marriage, that he had come to feel, as she did, that he wanted to spend the rest of their lives together, but not in the open relationship he was now suggesting.

She succeeded in pulling free of him and fled into the bathroom, locking the door against him.

'Zara! Damn it! Come here! Be sensible!' He hammered on the door, continuing his protests.

'I want you to go away,' she told him tautly. 'Get out of my flat and don't come back.' She could never work with Tor now. It would be too mortifying, now that he knew she had expected marriage, when it had still been the thing farthest from his mind.

'Go away!' she repeated. 'I *hate* you. Do you hear me? I hate you.'

'Yes, I hear you, damn you . . . and all right. I'll go. But don't think you've heard the last of me. When you've had time to cool off, you'll realise you're over-reacting. That I'm right.'

Nor had she seen the last of Tor, even though, in a panic that she might not be able to resist his demands, she fled to her father's house for sanctuary.

'God knows what you expected to achieve by running away,' he said tautly, as he strode across the threshold of the Gloucestershire house. She had been so taken aback at seeing him that she hadn't had the wit to slam the door in his angry face.

'What did *you* hope to achieve by following me?' she retorted, trying desperately to disguise the pain she felt at the sight of him.

'You didn't imagine I'd just let you walk out of my life like that?'

Zara shivered, clasping her arms about herself, as though by so doing she could erase the memory of his arms. She didn't want him to stay, but she knew he wouldn't readily leave until he'd had his say.

'What do you think these last few weeks were all about?' he demanded.

'Originally it was business!' she snapped, stung to anger by his manner. 'Until you thought you saw the opportunity of combining business with pleasure.'

'Are you telling me your co-operation was unwilling, that you didn't enjoy what we shared? You know damned well you enjoyed every second . . . and you'd have gone on enjoying it, but for one thing.'

'Marriage!' she spat the word at him. 'That's what you mean, isn't it? That's what frightened you off. Well, it may surprise you to know that I believed you to have some gentlemanly instincts, that it never occurred to me that you'd . . . you'd . . .'

'Take you without the intention of putting a ring on your finger? Grow up, Zara. Not every hot-blooded affair leads to marriage . . . and ours *was* hot-blooded, wasn't it?' As he spoke his expression changed and she knew that the old awareness was growing between them and a sudden movement on his part made her step backwards, averting her face.

'No,' she said, her voice strained, 'don't come near me. Our . . . our friendship is over. I . . . I don't want to work with you, and I don't want to see you again.'

His hand shot out, wrenching her head round so that she had to face him, and she saw with fearful fascination that a pulse ticked in his temple, his mouth was drawn into taut, savage lines.

'I don't believe you,' he muttered.

'You'll have to, because you'll find I mean it. I shall ring Charlie Laing tomorrow. I shan't be signing the contract you asked him to draw up. You can find yourself another illustrator. Please go,' she went on coldly, 'I'm busy. I've a lot of work to catch up on, work neglected while I wasted my time on you.'

'Is that your last word?' His eyes smouldered green fire.

'Yes,' she said defiantly, though her heart, her body ached to give in, to tell him she wanted to be with him, to be loved by him unconditionally.

'Then I'll go, but not before I've had *my* last word.'

She had expected a tongue-lashing and that would have been bad enough. What she didn't expect was that he would grab her, lifting her hard against his muscular chest, her feet inches above the floor, his mouth seeking hers as her lips parted in a breathless protest, her resistance destroyed by the violence of his kiss. It was a long kiss, expressing a raw, sensuous need, telling her of his physical hunger, reminding her painfully of her own. Then, slowly, as though reluctant to release her, he let her slide the full length of his body, deliberately, wickedly letting her feel his arousal, his pulsating manhood.

'Be very sure of what you say, Zara,' he told her. 'Because if I walk out of here, now, it will be for good.'

She didn't answer. She couldn't. She felt as if words would choke her. She could only hold his gaze, willing her face not to crumple into piteous tearfulness.

With a thud that jarred her teeth, he set her back on her feet and walked out of the house, out of her life, and though she longed to call him back, seething pride prevented her. He had been frightening in his anger, but the sensations with which he left her frightened her more. How could she bear never to see him again? How could she go on, never knowing again the fulfilment of the desires he aroused in her?

CHAPTER SIX

It had been some days before Zara could bring herself to return to London. She was fearful of accidentally encountering Tor. But at last, for the sake of her work, she could procrastinate no longer.

To her relief, she learnt, from Charlie Laing, that Tor had left town. Less palatably, she listened to her agent's complaints about the opportunity she had refused.

'Now the illustrations will be done by someone else, someone who falls short of your standards. What happened between you two? I thought you were getting on famously.'

'Obviously not,' Zara returned tartly, 'since we're not going to collaborate.'

The days, weeks, passed wearily and if it hadn't been for the necessity to meet her commitments, Zara feared she might have weakened, gone in search of Tor, begged him for a continuation of their relationship, on *his* terms. Cooped up in her flat day after day, evening after evening, she became more and more dispirited and it was almost with relief that, one Friday, she opened the door to see Michael Dane confronting her.

'What happened to the author, Zara?' he asked, as she invited him in. 'I haven't seen him around here lately,' and, at her look of incredulity, 'I've spent a lot of time just watching your front door,

Zara, hoping I'd see you, but you haven't set foot over the threshold. Have you been ill?'

In her lowered state, his concern, his unswerving devotion touched Zara and weakly she allowed herself to be persuaded into dining with him, into admitting that she was no longer seeing Tor.

'Best cure for a broken romance is a new one,' Michael told her jubilantly, 'but in our case, an old one renewed.' And Zara hadn't the heart to tell him his hopes were in vain.

As the weeks passed and it seemed certain Tor had meant what he said, that he would never trouble her again, Zara allowed her friendship with Michael to drift on, too dispirited to make the effort to push him aside. After all, as Michael himself had said, he was an old friend and old friends had the same comfort as a pair of well-worn shoes, requiring no effort on her part to please other than to acquiesce in his plans for their dates together.

Zara had first met Michael Dane early in her career, at one of her exhibitions. He was tall, good looking in a hard kind of way and a fellow artist, he'd told her ... but, as it turned out, an artist of a very different calibre. Their friendship had continued for over a year. Michael definitely had a talent, but he seemed almost to despise it. Had he chosen to develop his skill, he could have achieved a certain success, but he was, on his own admission, too lazy to push, maintaining that his work was, as he put it, 'good enough'. Thus he would never be able to command the respect or the stature that Zara rapidly attained, nor live satisfactorily by his art.

But he had a compelling personality, an easy charm, when he cared to exert it, a zest for enjoyment, which made him good company, and Zara, busy with her work, hadn't troubled to look far beneath the surface of this pleasant-enough companion, until he'd begun to press her to marry him, and then, out of fairness to him, she had ended their relationship. Now it was on again and Michael was complacent.

'I knew you'd come to your senses. That author fellow was just playing with you, wasn't he? I recognised his type, when I saw him with you. You're *my* girl, Zara,' and he made a joke of it, but Zara sensed his seriousness. 'I don't intend to let you escape again.'

Zara knew then that she ought to call a halt, but before she could find the right opportunity to do so, the right words in which to tell Michael of her feelings, two events occurred which affected her decision. The most traumatic was the loss of her father, something so totally unforeseen that it shook Zara to the roots of her being. Her father had always seemed so fit, so healthy. He was all the family she had. How *could* he just die and leave her all alone, especially now when she needed loving advice, understanding? For to add to the grief of her loss, Zara had an increasing anxiety. She had lost count of dates and times, but she was almost certainly pregnant. In her love and willingness to give herself to Tor, it had never occurred to her to take precautions. Her ravaged emotions, her loneliness, her fear, made Zara less than clear-headed and when, after the funeral, as Michael supported her stumbling figure from the graveside, he repeated his unfailing proposal of marriage, blindly she accepted. At least she wouldn't be totally alone, at least her child would have a name. If it occurred to her to contact Tor, to tell him that she bore his child, to give him a chance to take responsibility for it, she thrust the idea aside. She wouldn't, couldn't use her condition as a weapon of emotional blackmail.

On the day of the wedding, Zara awoke to two realisations, that she had developed a particularly heavy cold, and that she was certainly not pregnant. She had been feeling physically below par for a few days. Secretly she'd entertained a fantasy, where Tor would appear, insist that the ceremony could not go through, that she must marry him. Later, she learnt that he had only returned to England on the day of the wedding, his whereabouts for the past weeks unknown even to Charlie, his agent.

The weather was dreadful and a steady rain was falling, as Zara and Charlie, who had agreed to give her away, set out for the church.

'Still not too late to change your mind,' Charlie Laing told her during the drive. 'Dane's not the man for you, and you know it. You should be marrying Endacott, shouldn't you?'

Mutely, Zara shook her head. Throughout all Charlie's inquisitive probing, she had refused to reveal to what extent the friendship between her and Tor had developed, on what rocks it had foundered.

During the service, Zara tried not to let her thoughts turn to Tor, but afterwards, as she stood on the steps, her hand through the arm of her new husband, she thought her feverish longings must have conjured up the man whom she still loved, in spite of everything, as she stared for a long, heart-shaking moment into a drawn face, pain-filled green eyes. Then he was gone, vanished into the crowd. Had she really seen him? If not, why were her legs shaking beneath the long, full skirt of her dress, the nausea rising in her throat, as the realisation came to her, too late, of just what she had done, how irrevocable a step she had taken. Why hadn't she waited a little longer to be sure of her condition? Why hadn't she given herself a little longer to get over the first shock of her father's untimely death?

But for Michael's sake, she made a determined effort to pull herself together, realising that the photographers were waiting. She had just adopted a smile, which felt as though carved in some rigid, unbending material, rather than the flesh of her own face, when there was a totally unexpected interruption and she felt Michael's forearm tense under her hand, as two large men powered their way through the wedding guests, towards the bridal couple.

A newly married, bewildered Zara witnessed the arrest of her husband. Dazed, she listened to the charges ... robbery with violence ... and murder. At first she couldn't believe it, thought it must be a case of mistaken identity.

Weeks later, in a crowded courtroom, she was forced to believe it. The proof was overwhelming. Before she'd come back into his life, Michael *had* carried out a series of armed robberies. He'd been having an affair with a female accomplice, who, on learning of his approaching marriage, had threatened to go to Zara with her story, and the woman had met a brutal end. Had Michael really thought he could get away with these crimes, or was he slightly insane? Remembering his determined obsession with her, Zara couldn't help wondering now about his mental state.

Sentence was pronounced, life imprisonment, committal to Princetown on Dartmoor. Sitting beside Charlie Laing, who had offered himself as moral support, Zara watched her husband being led away between two police officers.

He turned to look at her, his cold blue eyes boring into hers across the heads of the sensation-seeking crowd, and Zara shivered convulsively. Despite the sentence, she had an overwhelming conviction that she hadn't seen or heard the last of Michael Dane.

'It's all over, Zara,' Charlie said comfortingly, his hand at her elbow.

'Is it?' she said dully.

'Yes, of course. He's going where he can't do any more harm.'

'I'm still married to him. Charlie, how could I have been so blind? Why didn't I realise what he was like? Am I such a bad judge of character?'

'No.' He squeezed her arm. 'He had us all fooled with that superficial charm of his. You mustn't blame yourself and if your judgment *was* a bit off, is it surprising, after all you've gone through, losing your father . . .?'

And losing Tor, she added silently, only Charlie didn't know about that. What she had finally convinced him was a breakdown in a business arrangement had had far more traumatic personal effects. She shivered as she thought of the future. What would become of her now? Even the thought of her work couldn't comfort her. Drearily, she allowed herself to be escorted, head bent to avoid the avid eyes of onlookers, so she did not see a familiar auburn head that towered above the crowd, did not intercept the sympathetic concern in the green eyes. Only afterwards did Charlie tell her that Tor had been in court.

'I believe he wanted to come over, but I shook my head at him. I didn't think you'd ... was I wrong?'

'You were quite right,' she told him. But there was a little pang of pain in the knowledge that Tor had been there and she hadn't noticed him. Surely her instincts should have told her that he was within her orbit? But she couldn't have faced him. She might have broken down and she didn't want his pity.

She was not to escape the vicinity of the law courts without one encounter. On the steps of the building, a couple approached her.

'Mrs Dane?'

She glanced up and but for Charlie's support might have fallen, so enormous was the shock. For a moment, she thought Michael had eluded his warders, but on closer inspection, she saw that this man was shorter, slighter, a paler reproduction of Michael Dane.

'Who ... who are you?' she whispered. But she knew, of course, a split second before he answered.

'Mike's brother. Syb and I should have been here for your wedding, but we had a last-minute hitch. We certainly didn't expect to walk into this little lot.'

Zara had known that Michael had a brother,

living in Australia, but not that they were twins.

'It must be awful for you,' she agreed in a low voice and at first she *had* felt sorry for Maurice Dane, newly returned to England for a reunion with his brother, only to find him arraigned for murder. She turned her attention to his wife, and, uncharacteristically for Zara, took an immediate dislike to the hard-faced, red-haired woman with thin lips and suspicious eyes. 'Are you staying in England long?' She hoped not. Her heart sank at Maurice's reply.

'We're here permanently. At least that *was* the idea. Mike reckoned, as he was settling down, it'd be nice if we could be nearby, me and Syb. A cosy sorta foursome, eh?'

Zara forced a polite smile.

'What will you do now?'

'Guess we'd better look around for a job of some sort. Pretty well drained our resources coming over.'

Should she offer them a loan, their passage back? Was that what they were expecting? All her instincts revolted against the idea of a transaction that would bind her to yet another Dane. Glad of Charlie still at her side, she held out her hand in a gesture of dismissal.

'Goodbye. I'm sorry we didn't meet under happier circumstances,' she forced herself to say.

'Do you *have* to rush off?' Maurice sounded aggrieved. 'I was sorta hoping we could chat, make some kinda plans . . .'

'Miss Sinclair . . . ah, Mrs Dane . . . has been through a considerable ordeal these past few weeks,' Charlie intervened. 'I think you must excuse her.'

For a moment, the blue eyes so like Michael's narrowed and hardened, and Zara sensed that the smile that followed was insincere.

'Course! Right you are! But can we look you up some time, whilst we're still in London?'

Zara hesitated. Her instincts told her it would be unwise to agree and yet her innate good breeding prevented her from outright refusal. Maurice seized upon this, thrusting a crumpled envelope into her hand.

'Just jot down your address, in case we have time to drop in on you, eh?'

Unwillingly, she complied, then moved away again on Charlie's arm. As she did so, she heard Sybil Dane ask sharply,

'What d'you want to call on *her* for?'

'Just an idea, Syb,' was the reply, before distance cut off the rest of his words.

Heaven only knew what sort of person the Danes had expected her to be, tarred with the same brush as Michael and themselves perhaps? They'd been wrong, and Zara let them know it, the day they called round at her flat, about a fortnight after their first encounter. She had been working hard, having taken Charlie's advice and immersed herself in a backlog of illustrative work. Even so, she couldn't do this without a pang at the reflection that she might instead have been illustrating Tor's book.

As well as her neglected commissions, new ones continually arrived on her desk. Only that morning, she'd received a request, via her agent, which normally would have made a tremendous appeal. T. Brett, as the writer signed himself, or herself, Zara wasn't sure which, was currently looking for an illustrator to collaborate on a new book. The letter came from a London address, but without going into too much detail, described an isolated country house, and mentioned the fact that an odd-job man and a secretary-cum-housekeeper were also required. If Miss Sinclair could personally recommend such persons, T. Brett would be grateful for her help. At the time, Zara had never dreamt that T. Brett was Tor, using his middle name as a pseudonym, trying to lure her to meet him, something he was certain she would not do voluntarily. But in any case, the isolated situation, the work offered, were too reminiscent of what might have been and she pencilled in a polite refusal, intending to type it out later, when she was less frantically busy.

Being so fully occupied, she wasn't pleased, therefore, when her doorbell sounded, and she was very tempted not to answer. But throwing down her pen and passing a hand over hair which she tended to ruffle during moments of concentration, she went to the door. She was even less pleased when she recognised Maurice and Sybil Dane, and realised that they expected to be asked in.

'I can spare you just half an hour,' she said bluntly. 'I have a deadline for this work.' An ink-stained hand indicated the jumble of papers on her desk.

The Danes, she noticed, were avidly taking in every detail of her well appointed apartment, noting the fact that the desk was an antique, the looking-glass Chippendale. They couldn't fail to realise that she was comfortably off, and the knowledge made her, somehow, uneasy.

'What can I do for you?' she asked, trying to hide her irritation at their blatant curiosity.

'We felt we ought to get to know Mike's wife.' Unexpectedly, it was Sybil who replied, sitting down with the air of one completely at home and intent upon remaining. Maurice, on the other hand, though he followed suit, seemed more tense, his blue eyes wary, defensive. 'We thought,' Sybil added, 'as his wife, you'd be keen to hear the latest about him, even though,' she added with heavy emphasis, 'you haven't tried to visit him yourself.'

'No.' Zara spoke coldly. She wasn't going to offer any excuses.

'But you will, of course, feel a moral obligation to *help* him,' Sybil stated, as if it were a certainty.

'Help him?' Zara stared. 'How can *I* help him?'

'You're a wealthy woman,' Maurice put in. 'Mike told us so, when he wrote.'

'Where he is, he won't need much money,' Zara said drily. .

'There *is* a way money could help.' Maurice leant forward. 'Look, aren't you even going to offer us a coffee while we talk?'

Zara hesitated. She didn't want to do anything to prolong the Danes' visit, nor did she want to talk about Michael. But once again good manners prevailed.

'Certainly you can have a coffee, but I'd appreciate it if you'd be brief. I really am busy.'

In the kitchen, as she made three cups of instant coffee, she found her hands were trembling. To offer the percolated variety would take longer, and suddenly, desperately, she wanted the Danes out of her flat. Even then she must have had a premonition. She drank her own coffee hurriedly, hoping her unwanted guests would do the same, but Maurice seemed determined not to be hurried, though he did come straight to the point.

'We need money to help us finance Mike's escape,' he said bluntly.

'What?' Zara was incredulous. 'You can't be serious?'

'Deadly serious. We visited Mike the day before yesterday and we agreed we'd try and get him out of that place, and we will, with your help.'

'It's quite impossible,' she said flatly. 'You'll never get him out and even if there were a chance, I couldn't, *wouldn't* help you.'

'But he's your husband . . .'

'Let's get this straight.' Zara was getting angry. 'Michael is my husband, but he wouldn't have been, if I'd had any idea what he was really like . . .'

'Listen to me, you disloyal, unfeeling little bitch.' Zara was treated to a sight of the Dane temperament, as Maurice leapt to his feet, towering over her in an intimidating fashion, in his anger sweeping all her drawings and correspondence to the floor. His hard-faced wife looked on, a contemptuous smile on her lips for Zara's ashen face. 'Listen to me, we're not leaving this country until we get what we came for, and now that includes springing Mike. When he wrote and told us to get on over here and share in his "good fortune", we thought he'd found himself someone like my Syb here. Syb'd share her last penny with me, if she had one.'

'I see,' anger replaced fear, 'so your precious brother invited you to come over and sponge off me?'

'Too right. There's too much damned unfair distribution of wealth in this world. Mike and I had it hard as kids, pulled ourselves up by our bootstraps. But what good did it do us? I went to Australia in the end, to see if I could make it out there, but Mike had the right idea. This country owed him a living, so he helped himself to what the privileged classes were holding on to.'

'I suppose,' Zara said sarcastically, 'that's why he knocked poor little old men on the head, for their hard-earned savings ... because they were so privileged.'

'Look, you snotty-nosed bitch.' Maurice's hand was on her shoulder now and he was hurting her. 'You make a mint of money with your scribbles. Mike told us. And you've inherited all your old man's cash now. You wouldn't even notice the little it'd take to get Mike out and ...'

'By bribery, I suppose? Because that's the only way.'

'Never you mind the whys and wherefores. We need money and you're going to supply it.' His fair complexion was suffused with angry blood. Zara thought he was going to strike her, and she was surprised when Sybil intervened. She'd believed the other woman to be the harder of the pair.

'Suppose we let Zara think it over, Mo?' she suggested. 'You've rushed her a mite. Suppose we come back, this time next week ...'

'It won't make any difference,' Zara informed

her, 'and besides, I shall tell the police what you've . . .'

'It'll only be your word,' Sybil reminded her, 'you've no concrete evidence.'

'I still think we should screw the money out of the little bitch,' Maurice muttered, but he responded to Sybil's hand on his arm.

'We'll see. Come on, Mo. There's always Plan B, *now*!'

Zara was so relieved to see the back of the couple, that she didn't even wonder what Plan B might be, though she was to discover soon enough. Sufficient for her that they *had* an alternative source of money. She knew she had nothing to support her story if she should contact the police.

Unable to concentrate any more on her creative work, she picked up her scattered papers and settled down instead to answer her neglected correspondence. Strangely enough, she couldn't find the letter from T. Brett. It must have become mixed up with everything else, when Maurice had swept the papers to the floor. She shrugged. It didn't much matter. T. Brett would just have to wait a little longer for the letter of refusal.

Incredibly, during the next two weeks, Zara had managed to forget Maurice and Sybil Dane. With a great concentration of will and effort, she succeeded in putting everything else to the back of her mind, as she dealt with her tremendous backlog of work and eventually her desk began to take on some semblance of normality, though she was puzzled when the unanswered letter never came to light.

Of course there were times when her personal problems rose to haunt her, usually in the small hours between midnight and dawn, when depression seemed most virulent, and she most vulnerable. But with daylight, there was always a resurgence of courage, a renewal of pride. She had made a mistake in marrying Michael, but she had made a far worse mistake when she'd given herself, body, heart and soul to Tor Endacott.

Apart from the fact of her marriage, life seemed almost normal again. She was working office-hours by day, relaxing, or endeavouring to do so, in the evenings, unless a particularly absorbing piece of work overran, and then it was a pleasure rather than a chore to work late, sometimes even into the small hours of the next day. It was just such a project that was occupying her, very early one Saturday morning, when the doorbell rang, a short, tentative sound, a secretive sound, so that in her concentration, she almost missed its summons.

'Who on earth?' she muttered, glancing at her wrist watch. 'Three a.m.?' She gave an exasperated sigh, knowing that now her mood was broken, she wouldn't be able to resume that particular project, even when the interruption had been dealt with.

'Do you realise what time it is?' she asked indignantly, a few moments later, as Maurice and Sybil Dane, without waiting for an invitation, pressed forward over the threshold. 'It's only by chance that I'm not in bed.'

'Never mind the time.' Maurice was brusque, with not even the pretence of politeness. It was as though the aggressive manner of their parting had been carried over to this moment. 'There are things to be settled.'

Suddenly Zara had a sensation of being menaced, as the Danes forced her to back into her study-cum-sitting-room and closed the door.

'Wh . . . what do you want?'

'We've seen Mike again, and it's all arranged,' Maurice told her, an air of triumphant truculence about him.

'You . . . you mean . . .' Zara's lips were dry. *Could* Maurice achieve his brother's escape, and if so, what would that mean for her?

'Yes, the escape . . . not the exact date yet, but the method is settled. You'll provide the means.'

'Count me out,' Zara interrupted.

''Fraid not!' His smile was a sinister twist of the weak, but rather sensual mouth. 'The three of us are going to be on the spot when it happens. Mike wants *you* there. So pack a bag, Zara. You're going with us . . . now.'

'I most certainly am not.' She moved towards her desk and the telephone. 'I'll give the pair of you two minutes to get out of here or . . .'

'Or what?' Maurice sneered, as a casual movement of his hand revealed his possession of a gun; a small one, but nonetheless deadly looking.

'Don't be a fool.' She tried to hide her fear. 'You wouldn't dare use that thing.'

'Try me,' Maurice invited. 'All you have to do is dial.' She heard the click as he removed the safety catch. 'Get her keys, Syb.'

Trembling with mingled fear and outrage, Zara watched as her handbag was upended, the contents spilling on to the desk, and the other woman held aloft a bunch of keys, which included that of Zara's Mini.

'Cheque book, credit cards and any loose cash,' Maurice ordered, and Sybil added these to her haul.

'What ... what happened to plan B?' Zara asked.

'You're it,' Sybil told her succinctly, 'that, and a certain letter from a T. Brett.'

'Brett?' The name struck a chord ... of course ... 'You mean *you* took my letter?'

'Explanations later,' Maurice snapped. 'Start packing!'

Zara would have protested further, but she knew she couldn't outwit two people and though she was no coward, she dared not call Maurice's bluff. He might just be desperate enough to wound her, even if not to kill her. To sustain injury or to lose her life would profit her nothing. But, fit and well, there might be an opportunity for her to thwart the Danes' plans. With the two of them standing over her, she threw a few essentials into a suitcase, hating the knowledge of their hard, prying, avaricious eyes, taking in every detail of her possessions, her intimate apparel.

'Classy stuff,' Sybil observed, her manner a mixture of disdain and envy. 'Anyone can look good, if they can afford to dress like that.'

'No wonder Mike's feeling a little frustrated,' Maurice drawled, stepping forward to finger a lacy slip.

Zara shuddered, but, surprisingly, it was Sybil who voiced the objection, slapping her husband's hand aside, telling him sharply that it was time they were on their way, before the streets below filled with people. The couple must have laid their plans carefully, for they hustled her down the rear fire escape, which emerged into a mews, making unerringly for the garage where Zara kept her car.

'This won't do you any good,' she told them, as they drove out into the early morning city.

'No?' Maurice grunted. 'I want you where I can keep an eye on you, while we're getting Mike out of that hell-hole.'

'And afterwards?' she had to ask.

'That's up to him. Back to Aussie, maybe. In any event, he wants you with us. Mike doesn't let go easily, as you'll find out.'

They drove all that day. Maurice was a nervous driver and despite Sybil's urging that he should 'put his foot down for God's sake,' they made poor time. Finally, as the afternoon light began to fade, the couple began to wrangle over the wisdom of going to an hotel, or of passing the night in the car. Sybil didn't relish the idea of Maurice driving on Dartmoor in the dark.

'And I don't see why we should have to rough it, just because of her,' Sybil went on. 'It's too damn cold this time of year to sleep out. We can take it in turns to keep an eye on her,' and then, as Maurice muttered about the expense, 'We should worry, she'll be paying.'

Eventually, the couple settled for a small country pub just beyond Taunton. As it was out of season, they had no difficulty in getting two rooms, a double to accommodate Zara and whoever was on guard, and a single one, which Maurice and Sybil would use in turn. With the

Danes on either side of her and that unseen but still present gun in Maurice's possession, there was no way Zara dared appeal to the proprietor for help. Since Maurice was worn out by the strain of exercising his indifferent driving skills, Sybil offered to take the first watch.

'Shouldn't we tie her up or something?' Maurice suggested, hovering uncertainly in the doorway.

'Use your wits! Suppose one of the staff came in? Don't worry,' Sybil adjured him grimly, 'she won't get away from *me*. Get some rest, Mo, and stop worrying.'

Zara studied her jailer. Sybil had thrown herself into the bedroom's only easy chair and looked totally relaxed, the brown, pebble-hard eyes wide open and alert. Both the Danes were greedy and acquisitive. Could she bribe the woman to let her go? She sat up on the bed to which Maurice had ordered her.

'Why are you doing this?' she asked Sybil. 'I can understand Maurice wanting to help his brother, but Michael is nothing to you, and if you're caught, it'll mean prison for you too.'

'Prison?' Sybil shrugged. 'Not if we're careful, and we shall be. But poverty is worse. You wouldn't know anything about that, with your big country mansion, your London flat *and* a career to boot. You've never had to go without.'

'You have?'

'Too right! Born in a slum, brought up in it until I was old enough to escape, working for other people for a miserable pittance and then,' she laughed sardonically, 'I go and fall for a man without two pennies to bless himself with. Then Australia! The land of opportunity! Maybe it is, for some, but not for the Danes, not without some money to invest.'

'You don't have to resort to crime to get money,' Zara told her eagerly, 'I could make it worth your while if you let me go now. Michael and Maurice need never know. We could make it look as if . . .'

'Forget it!' Sybil snapped. 'I don't intend to let *my* husband down, and as for making it worth my while, we'll be living off your money anyway.'

The other woman enlarged upon their plans. Once Michael was free, Zara would still be their prisoner, forced to accede to their demands for money, their intention, once the initial hue and cry had died down, being to return to Australia.

'But where does my letter come into all this? The letter from T. Brett?'

'Very convenient that,' Sybil mused, 'that Maurice should have spotted that letter. Useful that the Brett fellow . . . that's not his *real* name incidentally . . . should be looking for a whole household of staff, and as a bonus his place is very nicely situated too! So,' she sneered, 'you can draw your pretty pictures for him and Maurice and I can get on with our plans.'

'You mean you actually applied for those jobs, used my name? What makes you think I'll meekly work for this man, that I won't say anything to him about what you're up to?'

'Because,' there was a sinister threat underlying Sybil's reply, 'because you enjoy life, Zara Dane, and it wouldn't be healthy for you to double-cross us, any of us. Remember that other woman who tried to cross Mike? We shall be watching and listening the whole time.'

Sybil was over confident, Zara tried to reassure herself. Twenty-four-hour vigilance would be impossible. This man Brett . . . what *was* his real name, and why had he written to her under an alias? . . . surely he would be prepared to help her if he knew the truth? This idea was encouraged, when Sybil went on to tell Zara just who T. Brett really was. Despite her present perilous situation, Zara felt a thrill of joy run through her. Tor must still have some interest in her, to attempt to employ her once more. But surely, whatever his personal feelings, he wouldn't refuse to help her escape the Danes' clutches?

She closed her eyes. No use pleading or reasoning further with Sybil. Pretence became reality and when she opened her eyes again, it was to see a shirt-sleeved Maurice occupying the armchair. His jacket was slung over the back of the chair, his shoes down by its side. He was reading and hadn't noticed she was awake. Through lowered lashes, she studied him, his likeness to Michael, that same sensuality of features, noticing too the signs of weakness which Michael had never betrayed. Weak Maurice might be, but Zara knew it was no use trying on him the tactics she'd tried with Sybil. As Michael's twin, he had an even greater incentive than greed to help the escape.

As she watched, she noticed he was finding it increasingly difficult to concentrate on his newspaper, that more and more frequently, his eyelids drooped, so that every so often he came to with a little jerk, his eyes darting first towards the bed where she lay, then looking back at his paper. Avidly, she watched his attempts to stay awake.

His eyes remained closed for longer and longer periods, and there came the moment when a gentle snore betrayed the fact that he was soundly asleep.

Zara assessed the distance she must cross to reach the door, visualised the layout of the building, the whereabouts in the car-park of her car. To use it as a means of escape, she had first to obtain the keys. Let them be in Maurice's pocket, she begged inwardly, let me get my hands on them.

Still watching the sleeping man, she sat up cautiously, gained the edge of the bed, picked up her shoes and began to move step by step towards the somnolent figure. Once he snorted and moved restlessly, so that she froze on the spot. But he settled again.

His head was resting on his jacket, but, to Zara's relief, the pockets were accessible. Slowly, carefully, she slid her hand into one pocket, then the other. Success. Gingerly, she withdrew the bunch of keys, keeping her gaze on Maurice's sleep-slackened face.

Now she moved towards the door, turned the handle, opened the door just sufficiently to allow her to slide out on to the darkened landing. She hurried along the corridor and down the stairs. Maurice could wake at any moment and would be hot on her heels. The building was in total silence, as she shot back the heavy bolt of the outer door and stepped into the yard. A short distance to the car and she unlocked it, scrambled into the driving seat, not even pausing to put on her shoes.

It was not quite light and a thin mist obscured

the countryside, a mist which had dampened the
Mini's engine. At the first attempt it refused to
fire and as she tried for the second time, her teeth
clenched agonisingly on her bottom lip, she heard
a wild yell of rage, saw Maurice emerge from the
building. Another frantic attempt, and the engine
sprang to life. She engaged second gear and
accelerated madly, the choke pulled right out, as
she headed for the exit. She was so terrified that
even now Maurice might come up with her, that
she looked neither to right nor to left, so that the
lone, early motorist took her by surprise. Too
late, she tried to brake, felt her stockinged feet
slip on the pedal. She wrenched the wheel hard
over and missed the other car, but crashed the
Mini into the wall and everything ceased to exist
... until they told her that her name was Zara
Dane, that she was twenty-three years old, and a
married woman.

Her car! She'd wrecked her own car, not
Maurice's! Another lie! How relieved the
accomplices must have been when her accident
resulted in amnesia. How swiftly they must have
adjusted their plans. Only one of the tales they'd
told her had been true. They *had* obtained
employment with Tor Endacott, but not via any
advertisement. What must Tor have thought
when he'd received the forged reply to his letter,
forged in Zara's name? And what had he hoped to
achieve by tricking her into meeting him? It
could only be her collaboration. He knew she was
married, knew of the sequel to that marriage.
   Even so, despite her present danger, Zara's
pulses leapt. No wonder her senses, her whole

self had responded so ardently to Tor's love-making. He was the man she had once hoped to marry. No wonder he'd been stunned to find that she'd lost her memory, believed herself to be *Maurice's* wife. But how could he have imagined her to be faking her condition? Had he suspected her of complicity in the Danes' plans, believed she was making use of her knowledge of Wolfstor Farm, and him, that she too desired Michael's escape? That would account for his continuing flashes of hostility, even after he'd been forced to believe in her amnesia.

But why had Tor employed the *three* of them? It didn't make sense. He hated the idea of servants around the place when he was working. Unless . . . was it because he'd recognised the name Dane, suspected Maurice's motives for wanting to work so near to the prison? It was the only logical explanation.

Zara moved swiftly through the farmhouse, heading first for Tor's rooms. He and Michael were much of a size. She hated the idea of Michael using Tor's things, but she dared not disobey her husband. The clothing problem settled, she made a hasty tour of the house. It was deserted. This put a slightly different complexion on things. If Maurice had been here, he would have reinforced Michael's commands, and Zara would have stood no chance of outwitting the pair of them. But the house was empty, Michael on the outside, and she was indoors! If she could bolt the back door . . .

CHAPTER SEVEN

HEART thumping, every nerve quivering, Zara stole downstairs, through the empty house and into the kitchen. All was as it had been before, the only movement the slight lift and fall of the saucepan lid, from beneath which wafted the steaming odour of hotpot. Though Michael could not possibly hear her, she tiptoed towards the back door, and had shot the heavy bolts at top and bottom, when a sound made her whirl around to see him watching her.

'How ... how ...?' she stammered.

Two giant strides brought him to her side.

'Double-crossing bitch!' he said savagely and the back of his hand caught her across the face, his knuckles connecting with her cheekbone. 'Though you'd keep me out, did you? Good thing I decided to check up on you.' He inspected the slacks and sweater she had brought downstairs, then turned his attention to the contents of the saucepan. 'A plate!' he snapped.

'Sh ... shouldn't you be on your way?' she suggested nervously. She was terrified Tor would return and of what might happen if he did.

'I don't see why. I don't know where the owner of this place has got to, but we're on the inside and he's not. It's warm and comfortable after that blasted moor. I've got food, I've got you, and they'll never think of looking for me here.' He began to fill his mouth, more like a man who

144

hadn't eaten for days rather than a few hours. 'Sit down, there, where I can see you.' He pointed to the seat immediately opposite him.

Sitting, watching him eat, Zara wondered what her life would have been like if Michael hadn't been arrested so soon after their wedding. Would he have revealed himself in his true colours like this, or would he have maintained his pretence? What would it have been like to live with him as his wife? She shuddered. Thank God that hadn't happened. Eventually, Michael pushed his plate away with a sigh of satisfaction.

'Bloody good! Mind you, anything would taste good outside of that place. It takes the edge off your appetite, when you realise where you are.' Suddenly he struck his hand violently on the edge of the table. 'And I'm not going back inside. D'you hear me, Zara?'

Speechlessly, she nodded. She believed him. But to what lengths would he go, to ensure that he wasn't recaptured?

'We'll stay here tonight,' he announced after a moment or two. 'By morning the search will have moved further away. Now make me a coffee.'

Silently she moved to do his bidding. How could she persuade him to move on before Tor returned, as he soon must? She didn't relish spending the night here, alone with Michael. He'd never really loved her, as he'd claimed to do. Even if Sybil had not revealed the truth so brutally, she would have guessed for herself by now that though Michael desired her, he desired her money even more. But suppose he decided to take up their relationship where it had left off? Nauseated, she closed her eyes and swayed, clutching at the stove for support.

'Hurry up with that coffee!' Michael leant back in his chair and began to roll a cigarette. She watched his movements, the selection of a thin thread of loose tobacco, the expert flick of the paper, precise, delicate licking of its gummed edge. 'You learn to be economical with smokes inside,' he told her. 'Any decent cigarettes in the house?'

At first Zara shook her head. Tor didn't smoke. Then she remembered that Maurice did, and with the remembrance came the thought of the bathroom adjoining the room she and Maurice shared. It had a solid door and a sturdy bolt. If she could get to that door, get it between her and Michael . . .

'There may be some upstairs,' she offered, 'Maurice smokes. Shall I . . .?'

'We'll both go,' he asserted grimly and Zara's heart sank. Michael would be difficult, perhaps impossible to fool.

Avidly, it seemed to Zara, he took in the details of the bedroom, his eyes going immediately to the single beds.

'No double bed, eh?' His eyes were hard as he held Zara's unwilling gaze. 'Ever share either of these?'

If Maurice had been present, she would have lied valiantly, hoping to set the twins against each other. But there was no point in arousing an antagonism which would be directed solely against her.

'No,' she said firmly, then 'Maurice . . . Maurice was too . . . too considerate. He thought, as I'd lost my memory . . .'

'That's fortunate, for both of you,' Michael said

with an inflexion that made her shudder. 'So,' his gaze became reflective, 'you're still untouched?'

Zara didn't answer, she couldn't truthfully say yes, but she didn't need to. Her silence gave assent and she was aware of Michael storing up the information for future reference. She shuddered.

An unopened pack of cigarettes in his pocket, Michael now took time to study the layout of the rest of the house, reassuring himself that the front door too was bolted. The windows, he soon discovered, could be reinforced by sturdy internal shutters, made to withstand penetrating moorland winds.

'Does Endacott keep any firearms about the place?' he demanded and Zara shook her head. Thank goodness he didn't. The idea of Michael with a lethal weapon to handle was a frightening one. 'No gun, eh? Oh well, there's more than one way of skinning a cat.' With this obscure remark, he motioned her into the sitting-room and stretched himself out full length on the settee. Zara winced to see his dirty shoes on the upholstery, but she dared not protest. Besides, if he relaxed sufficiently, he might fall asleep and . . . It was as if her thought transmitted itself to his cunning brain. 'Don't get excited. I shan't drop off. I can go for a long time without sleep.' He studied her, then: 'It's been quite a while since I had the company of an attractive woman, and you *are* attractive to men, aren't you, Zara? What's this Endacott fellow like? Old, young?'

'Oh, middling,' she said vaguely, deliberately infusing a lack of interest into her tone.

'Lost your interest in men as well as your

memory,' he sneered. 'Where is Endacott anyway?'

'I don't know,' she said truthfully.

'Good. Let's hope he won't be back tonight. Maybe Maurice managed to get him out of the way. Perhaps he got *something* right.'

There was silence, the utter silence of the moorland night, whilst the fire crackled in the open grate. Then came the sound of hoofs striking the cobbled approach to the house. Tor's pony? What would happen when Tor found his own house locked and bolted against him, windows shuttered? He was bound to realise something was afoot, and being astute would probably guess just what it was.

Michael too had heard the pony's approach and he had risen from the settee, going to stand in the doorway that connected with the kitchen, where he stood, tense, alert. The back door rattled slightly, as if someone had attempted to turn the handle, then came the unmistakable sound of a key being inserted in the lock. But the door held fast. Muffled by the heavy timbers, Zara heard Tor's voice.

'Zara? Are you there? It's me, Tor!'

Michael was at her side immediately, one arm clamped about her, his hand over her mouth.

'Is that Endacott?' he hissed and mutely, she nodded. 'Blast it! He's bound to get suspicious if we don't let him in. We don't want him charging off to get the law.' He wrenched Zara round to face him. 'Listen to me . . . you're going to open that door and let him in. I'll keep out of sight. What sort of fellow is he, physically?'

'Big, strong,' she said hastily. 'I wouldn't risk it if I were you.'

'It's a risk I'll have to take. Next time he calls out, answer him. Open the door slowly and carefully, and no tricks.'

In tense silence, they waited. Would Tor call again, could she, dared she warn him?

'Zara, can you hear me? Are you all right?'

'Go on,' Michael ordered. 'Do it, just like I said. Now!' Roughly, he thrust her towards the door and took up his position. She reached up for the top bolt, making a great show of difficulty in sliding it back. Then she stooped to the bottom bolt. Now it was only a matter of turning the key and Tor would be inside and in danger. She couldn't do it. She would rather risk *her* life than his. A large, impatient hand snaked out from behind her, unlocking the door and as Tor, hearing the sound, surged forward, she screamed.

'No, don't come in. He's here . . . he'll . . .'

Then a vicious blow caught her on the side of the head, sending her sprawling.

She came to, her head pounding, the sour taste of blood in her mouth where she had bitten her tongue. She couldn't move. Hands and feet were bound, the floor she lay on hard, despite its carpet. It was the sound of someone saying her name over and over again which had brought her to her senses. She opened her eyes, wincing as a bright light invaded her aching head. She was in the sitting-room and not far away from her, tied to a heavy chair, was Tor, his face bruised, cut and bleeding, his green eyes anxious.

'Oh, Tor!'

At the sound of her voice, he drew a breath a relief.

'Thank God. I thought the swine had killed you. Your warning came too late. Mind you, I don't know that I'd have heeded it anyway. I couldn't have left you alone with the brute. I rushed in, tripped over you and he clobbered me, very effectively. Then,' he added grimly, 'he took one look at me and he seemed to go berserk.'

'He did recognise you then,' Zara said dully.

'Recognised me?' Tor was suddenly alert, his eyes suspicious. 'What exactly do you mean?'

'He didn't know your name, but he saw you with me once, remember? He knew that you, that we . . . I . . .' Under the intent stare of those green eyes, she began to colour.

'So *you* know who I am?' he said, an odd note in his voice. 'Since when, may I ask?'

'Since I bumped into Michael, out there on the moor, and recognised *him*. Everything came back in a rush. Oh, Tor, what are we going to do? He's a desperate, dangerous man.'

'There's nothing we can do at the moment,' he told her, then savagely, 'What on earth possessed you to marry Dane? Had you no idea what he was like?' And as she shook her head, 'You must be a rotten judge of character.'

'Yes, I *must* be,' she said significantly, anger rising inside her despite her knowledge of their danger. The significance of her words was not lost on him.

'If that means what I think it means—' His face had darkened angrily. 'But there's nothing to be gained by fighting between ourselves. If and when we get out of here, there'll be time enough to sort out *our* differences.'

If she ever got out of this, Zara thought, she was going to put a great deal of distance between herself and Dartmoor, between herself and Tor Endacott. She never wanted to see him again, to be reminded of the part he had played in this episode of her life. It was partly his fault, she mused savagely, that she was in this situation.

'Why did you do it, Zara?' Tor asked suddenly. 'Why did you get involved in this mess? Did you really feel that much for Dane, that you wanted him back . . . a thug, a murderer? And what kind of sap did you take me for, thinking you could use my home as a base for your operations?'

'I didn't think that. It had nothing to do with me. I didn't know . . . at least . . .'

'Ah, now we come to it. I'm glad you haven't the brass to lie to me. When I got your letter, accepting the job I'd offered you, when I *saw* the names of the people you were recommending to me as household staff . . .!'

'I didn't write that letter,' she interrupted. 'Maurice saw yours one day, when he was at my flat, and took it on himself to accept on my behalf. I would have refused . . . and besides,' she added, 'how could I have known "T. Brett" was you?'

'Then how the hell did you eventually turn up here? Just what did happen? How *did* you lose your memory . . . *if you did*!'

It passed a little of the time, bringing Tor up to date, gave her satisfaction to see that he had to believe her indignant refutal of his accusations. But, her account finished, Zara began to worry again about their present situation, until, having heard the murmur of their voices, Michael returned.

'So *you're* awake again,' he observed to Zara.

'No thanks to you,' Tor snapped, before she could reply. 'You might have killed her.'

Michael aimed a savage kick at the other man's shin and Zara gasped in outraged sympathy, as she heard his foot in its heavy boot connect and saw Tor wince.

'There's no need for that,' she cried.

'No need?' Michael turned on her. 'Oh yes there is. Do you think I'm daft? I know who this blighter is.' He swung back to Tor. 'You needn't have worried yourself about Zara. She's quite safe in my hands. You see, I haven't finished with her yet. After all, she's my wife, and there's a little matter of a honeymoon we missed.'

Tor's face mirrored Zara's own revulsion, green eyes glittering, and she feared he would retort, incurring further violence from their unstable captor. But, with an obvious effort, he bit back the words.

'Right, Endacott,' Michael continued. 'Where's my brother got to?'

'How should Tor know that?' Zara intervened swiftly.

'I guess there's a lot he knows. A lot of things are beginning to fit together, now I know who he is. He took my brother for a sucker. He must have known all along who Maurice was.'

'Yes,' Tor said suddenly. 'I did, and the police know too. They've known all along. We set a trap, for the lot of you.'

'Why you . . .!' Michael uttered an unspeakable word, taking a step towards the other man, but Tor faced him unflinchingly.

'You might as well give yourself up, Dane.

Your brother and his wife are in police hands already. As soon as you made your break they were picked up. We knew, you see, that something like this was meant to happen, and if it hadn't been for the fog you wouldn't have got *this* far.'

'Tor,' Zara cried, 'if you knew, if the police knew, why didn't they stop him escaping?'

'Because until he did, they had nothing to charge his accomplices with. I'm sorry, Zara, that it turned out like this. It wasn't meant to.' He looked at Michael. 'But it's only a matter of time before they work out where you are. Why not accept the fact, man?'

'They won't get me back in there,' Michael said with conviction. 'I'll see you in hell first, the pair of you. But first,' and his hard blue eyes raked over Zara, a hot, sensual look that made her shiver, 'but first there's a little matter of something owing to me.'

'Dane!' Tor cried urgently, struggling against his bonds. 'If you lay a finger on her, I'll . . . I'll . . .'

'You'll what?' the other sneered. 'You're in no position to do anything . . . except watch!'

'No, oh no!' Zara gasped. 'You couldn't . . . you couldn't be so cruel . . . so . . . so disgusting!' But his expression told her that he could. He intended to take what he considered to be his rights as her husband and he was going to force Tor to witness his possession of her. Tears began to stream down her face at the thought of this brutal degradation, at its irrevocable effect on any remaining feeling Tor might have for her.

A steady flow of oaths and threats came from

Tor, the kind of language she had never heard on his lips, as Michael hauled her up from the floor and flung her on to the settee. As his hand went to the waistband of his trousers and his tongue moistened his full lips, Zara prayed that she might faint.

Then, an exterior sound made her heart surge in sudden hope. Somewhere, a loud, disembodied voice was speaking Michael's name. A loudspeaker! The police!

'We know you're in there, Dane. Give yourself up, or it'll be the worse for you.'

Michael hesitated. Underneath every bully and braggart there lay a coward, Zara thought, and now she saw that side of her husband's nature.

'Maybe there's a better use for you,' he muttered, his cold blue eyes on Zara's apprehensive face. He turned abruptly and strode from the room, and they heard him taking the stairs two at a time. There was the sound of an upper window opening and then Michael's voice, stentorian on the quiet moorland night.

'I've got two hostages in here. You'd better think twice before trying anything, unless you want two deaths on your conscience.'

'Don't be a fool, Dane,' came the reply.

'What's foolish about it?' he mocked. 'I've killed before. Two more will make no difference to me.'

Down below, the two people whose lives were at stake held their breath.

'What do you want, Dane?' The loudspeaker enquired after a few moments' considering silence.

'Safe conduct out of here. A car at the door, with its engine running, no interference, and the girl goes with me. After all, she's my wife.'

'Will they give him what he asks for?' Zara asked Tor, her blue-grey eyes wide with fear.

'I think that may be up to you,' he said slowly, his voice full of deep concern. 'Zara, I want you to know . . .'

'Bring your wife to the window,' the voice outside broke in upon their conversation, 'let her speak for herself.'

Heavy footsteps on the stairs, and then Zara was bundled up them and into the front bedroom.

'Mrs Dane?' the voice enquired. 'Are you all right?'

'So far,' she shouted, her tone bitter, 'apart from a few bruises.'

'Shut up!' Michael said savagely, his grasp endangering the fragile bones of her wrist. 'Co-operate, or I'll finish Endacott off before we leave here.'

'Are you willing to go with your husband, if we allow him to leave?'

'I don't seem to have much choice.' Her answer began bravely enough, but ended on a despairing sob.

'Is Mr Endacott all right?'

'He will be,' she said dully, 'if you let my husband go.'

There was a long, seemingly endless silence, as if many people discussed the pros and cons. Perhaps they couldn't agree. Perhaps their main concern was to recapture the escaped convict, rather than to save the life of his victims? Then, when it seemed the waiting would go on forever, came the decision.

'Right! There'll be a car at the rear door in five minutes. There will be no attempt to interfere with your escape.'

Freeing her feet so she could walk, Michael pushed Zara back downstairs.

'Say goodbye to your boyfriend,' he sneered, 'because this is the last you'll see of each other.' His cold blue eyes narrowed. 'I wonder if I oughtn't to finish him off anyway, before I go? It wouldn't make any difference.'

Zara sickened, her eyes going to Tor's face. If anything happened to him, her life would be meaningless. About to plead with Michael, she paused. To beg for Tor's life might well harden his resolution, if he believed she still cared for the other man. So, instead, knowing the risk she took, that her bluff might backfire, she shrugged.

'Just as you like, if you *want* to waste more time.'

She willed Tor to understand, but, at his incredulous look, she knew he hadn't. He believed she was indifferent to his fate and somewhere inside her something bled to death. Michael hesitated, then he grunted:

'You're probably right. Why waste time on him? Let him go on living, knowing you're with me. In the long run that'll be worse than death.'

As promised, a car was parked close to the rear entrance, doors open, engine running, and with swift, furtive glances about him, Michael emerged from the house, Zara held tightly against him, her body a shield for his. Though she too glanced desperately around her, there was no sign of anyone to come to her aid and she guessed they dared not, for her sake. Now Tor's safety was assured, a little of her old fighting spirit reasserted itself. Michael couldn't be on the alert forever. Someday, somehow, somewhere, she would escape him. For the present, she must seem to acquiesce.

Car doors slammed, gears were engaged and with a furious revving and spinning of wheels, they screeched out of the farmyard and away along the narrow track that led out to the moorland road. Zara twisted her neck for a long, last look at Wolfstor Farm. She would never see it again, but she would never forget it.

The fog had come down again and rain fell too, so that, after the first initial wild spurt of speed, it was impossible for Michael to drive very fast. He couldn't risk the car going off the road. It was his lifeline, and as he slowed for a tortuous hairpin bend in the track, which scarcely deserved the courtesy of being called a road, Zara was seized by a sudden desperate impulse. To think was to act, and in one fluid movement, her bound hands notwithstanding, she managed to thrust open the passenger door and flung herself outward, praying for a soft landing.

Then there was soft moorland turf beneath her, and though hampered by her bonds, she managed to roll on to her feet and stumble away, not knowing where she was, or where she might be heading, except that anywhere was better than being in the proximity of Michael Dane. She had banked on his being so anxious to escape that he would drive on, cutting his losses where she was concerned. But no. Her heart gave a wild leap of fear as she heard the car screech to a halt, heard the thud of heavy feet, as he came in determined pursuit of her. She ran forward into the fog, hoping its thick, grey tendrils would hide her from the eyes of her pursuer.

Once she fell, her ankle twisting beneath her, and from the stab of pain when she rose, she guessed she had damaged it. But somehow she contrived to stumble on, the superhuman effort it required prompted by her fear of the man who followed. She slithered down an incline and the sudden icy shock of water told her she had come across one of the streams that meandered here and there across the moor. She began to follow it, glad of the anesthetising effect of the cold water upon her painful ankle.

A bulky shape loomed up before her out of the mist and for a moment her heart almost failed her, as she thought her pursuer had got ahead of her. But it was only a bridge, a single-stone, clapper bridge, consisting of one immense slab, its buttresses of more rough, unhewn rock. Here was a refuge of a kind. She knew she couldn't struggle on much further. Was the water level low enough for her to conceal herself beneath the bridge? There *was* room, and a tuft of earth and grass, just large enough for her to be able to perch above water level.

Cold, shivering with fear and reaction, she crouched in the cramped space, heard Michael's pounding feet as he ran back and forth in search of her. If he found her now, her life wouldn't be worth a penny, so great must be his fury. But the footsteps gradually faded away and at last she could let out her breath on a series of racking sobs. Yet still she dared not move, in case he returned, or she blundered into him. She settled down for a long, uncomfortable wait.

Somehow, despite her precarious position, she must have dozed off, and her uneasy slumbers were punctuated by unpleasant nightmares. She woke once with a scream, stifled immediately, as she remembered where she was. Then came a sound that struck panic into her soul ... footsteps crunched on the stones of the track crossing the bridge. She froze against the rough stonework.

'Zara! Zara! For God's sake, if you're anywhere near, answer me.'

'Tor! Down here!' A shuddering moan of relief escaped her. She had sworn she never wanted to see him again, but now her resolve wavered. Then the glare of torchlight illuminated her, as Tor bent to peer beneath the bridge. Instantly, he was in the water, up to his knees, swearing long and hard at her pitiable condition.

'I've been out of my mind with worry, ever since the police found the car abandoned.'

So Michael too was still on the moor somewhere, still a danger to them.

'He would have killed me eventually, I know he would,' she sobbed distractedly, as Tor hauled her free from her refuge. 'I had to take the chance of escape.'

'Of course you did,' he said soothingly, then recommenced his bitter swearing, as he bent and lifted her sodden form, carrying her effortlessly over the ground which she had covered with so much pain and difficulty.

'How did you know where to find me?'

'I didn't. I've just been covering the ground in a wide area from where we found the car.'

'Do you . . . do you think he's got completely away?' She hoped so, not for Michael's sake, but for theirs, that they might not encounter him again.

'Looks like it,' he said tersely. 'The police are searching now though. But we have to get you home, before you catch pneumonia.'

'How long have you been looking for me?'

Tor was as thoroughly soaked as she, his auburn hair plastered to his head, his anorak heavy with rainwater.

'Ever since the police untied me . . . about three hours.'

'I'm . . . I'm sorry,' she began, intending to apologise for all the trouble she had brought to his home, however unwittingly, however unwillingly.

'Just be quiet and rest,' he commanded.

She closed her eyes, thankful to obey. The effort of speech was almost more than she could manage and she was grateful too for his comforting proximity.

Immediately they reached Wolfstor Farm, he carried her upstairs, not to the bathroom she'd shared with Maurice, but to his own, adjoining his bedroom. He deposited her in a chair and began at once to draw a hot bath. As the steam rose, it brought with it the heady aroma of a fragrant, masculine bath preparation. Tor stripped off his anorak and rolled up his sleeves, turned to face her, his expression that of someone determined to override any possible protests.

'Right!' he commanded, advancing upon her, his intent obvious.

'Oh no!' She shook her head, panicking badly. She couldn't let him touch her. 'I'll manage . . .

just leave me ... I ...'

'No way!' he said emphatically and to ensure her compliance, he pulled her to her feet, his fingers going immediately to the wool of her soaking sweater, pulling it ruthlessly over her head, then turning his attention to the equally sodden jeans.

She tried to twist away from him, the touch of his hands too evocative of past intimacies, when she had willingly allowed him to undress her, to seek, to caress, but the events of the past hours had sapped every ounce of her strength.

He was gentle with her, removing her remaining clothing, which didn't amount to much anyway, two negligible scraps of lace. Then he lifted her and lowered her into the embrace of the essence-softened water and with a little sigh, she relaxed, letting the soothing warmth sweep over her.

She had expected that he would leave her now and her eyes widened apprehensively, as he bent over her, lathering the soap between his strong hands. Then those hands were moving slowly over her body, missing no part of it, massaging the warmth and life back into her, and arousing other numbed sensations to intolerable heights. Once she dared to glance at him, then looked swiftly away, his expression was too revealing. The ministrations he was performing for her were affecting him deeply.

But just as she felt she could bear his insidious attentions no longer, he lifted her out and then proceeded to dry her with the same tender thoroughness, a proceeding which rendered her even more incapable of resistance.

'Feeling warmer now?' he enquired solicitously, yet with a huskiness, a hint of suggestiveness in his voice, which made it plain that he expected his attentions to have thawed more than her outer being.

'Y . . . yes, thank you.' She could not meet his eyes again, in case he recognised the extent of his effect upon her. She didn't want any revival of that chemistry which had once so emphatically surged between them. Life was already too complicated.

He carried her back into his bedroom and wrapped her in his own dressing gown, the material redolent of his distinctive masculine fragrance. She noticed now that he too looked unutterably weary, that he still wore his own wet, mud-spattered clothing. Concern for him banished lethargy.

'You must have a bath too,' she told him. 'Or you'll get chilled.'

Momentarily his eyes gleamed.

'Will *you* bath *me*?'

'Oh . . .' She swallowed convulsively, imagining, longing. 'I . . . I couldn't,' she protested. 'I'd . . . I'd rather not,' she ended weakly.

'Very well.' His tone was dull as he turned towards the bathroom once more. 'Wait there. I shan't be long.'

As the door closed behind him, she sank on to the edge of the bed, gazing blindly before her. The euphoria induced by her rescue, the sense of well-being restored by the bath, began to fade. It was no use deluding herself. Her problems were not resolved, far from it. True, she'd regained her memory, though the recall had not been under pleasant circumstances. Maurice and Sybil were out of her life, but she was still married to Michael, a convicted criminal, still at large, still somewhere on the moor.

Suppose he returned here, to the farmhouse? A wave of panic swept through her. Had Tor bolted the door when they came in, or had he forgotten, in his concentration on getting her to a warm bath? She couldn't remember. But she couldn't sit here and wait until he'd finished his bath. That might be too late. She had to know that the house was secure against intruders ... one particular intruder.

Fear must have dulled her wits, she thought later, since it never even occurred to her to call her question through the closed door. Instead, heart in mouth, she stole downstairs and into the kitchen. Surprising how weak her legs still felt, and her ankle ached abominably, but at least it wasn't broken. Somehow she managed to reach the door, then gave a great sigh of relief. It was both locked and bolted.

The effort had sapped her little remaining strength and she slid down against the solid timbers, feeling the coldness of the flags against her bare legs, but unable to do anything about the discomfort.

'What the hell are you trying to do now?' Tor stood in the kitchen doorway, a towel wound sarong-wise about his hips, his upper torso bare, save for the strong growth of auburn hair that roughened its surface.

'I ... I wanted to be sure the door was locked,' she explained weakly, as he retrieved her from her slumped position, holding her to his naked chest, so that she felt the brush of its downy covering against her cheek.

His reply, as he carried her back towards the staircase, was scornful.

'Did you really think I'd be fool enough to neglect that precaution?'

'I'm so afraid Michael might come back for me,' she confessed, but somehow her fear had lessened. The sensation of being held securely in his arms once more was pervading her being with other emotions, far more pleasant, a series of delicious little tremors.

'He'd have to use a sledge hammer to get at you again,' Tor reassured her as he re-entered the bedroom and deposited her carefully on the bed. 'And he'd have *me* to deal with. He wouldn't take me by surprise a second time. He's not getting you away from me ever again.'

She stared up at him, her eyes clouding over. Didn't he realise? It wasn't just a question of taking her away. Michael Dane had just as sure a way of coming between her and Tor. Even if Tor *had* been the marrying kind, Michael was her husband . . . at least, until she could obtain a divorce, for that was what she wanted to do now. But how did you set about divorcing a man whose whereabouts you didn't know? And after the divorce, what then? Tor had made his feelings pretty clear right from the start. Besides, Zara wasn't even sure that she herself would risk entering into marriage a second time. One disastrous experience was enough. The best thing she could do, when she got away from here, was to put all thoughts of men behind her and concentrate on her career.

To put thoughts of one particular man behind her was easier said than done, her thudding heart told her, as Tor sat on the edge of the bed, leaning over her, his startling green eyes intent upon her face.

'I'm glad your memory's returned,' he said at length, then, a wry smile creasing his attractive face, 'I was getting tired of experiments. Perhaps now we can concentrate on the real thing?' And he moved closer. But she evaded him, sliding across the bed, one hand tugging at the hem of the very inadequate robe he'd lent her.

'No,' she said firmly.

Immediately his face darkened.

'Why?' he demanded. 'You know now who I am, what we were to each other.'

'We were never anything to each other,' she contradicted, at least, she amended inwardly, she hadn't meant to him all the things that *he* had come to mean to her. Tor misunderstood her denial, his eyes turning almost black with anger.

'You're not still infatuated with Dane? You can't be, not after all that's happened?' His eyes narrowed. 'I know some women have a masochistic desire to be treated brutally. Is that how it is with you? Was that his appeal for you. If so . . .'

'No!' She shook her head vigorously, but he swept on, anger, resentment riding him.

'You made no protest, did you, no attempt to prevent him, when he contemplated violence on me, before leaving here?'

She'd known then he would misunderstand her reaction and she hastened to clarify matters, her tongue stumbling over the words.

'No, Tor, no, it wasn't like that. I knew any

opposition would make him more determined, that if he thought I cared what . . . what . . .' She stopped, confused, as the green eyes softened, warmed.

'So that's how it was,' he murmured, 'and I thought you were indifferent to my fate.'

'Oh no.' Colour suffused her cheeks, as she whispered the words. 'I couldn't have borne it, if he'd . . . he'd . . .' Her words faltered away before the growing gleam in his eyes.

'Then you *do* care!' It was an exultant statement of fact. With a sudden movement, taking her unprepared, his arms clamped around her, his lips pressed against the soft fresh skin of her throat.

'Tor, I . . .' She began to protest, but she was trembling violently, under the touch of his firm, warm mouth, as his hands slid beneath the robe she wore to cup and caress her breasts.

'Kiss me, Zara!' It was a command, but he did not wait for her compliance, forcing her mouth open with his own, possessing hers hotly. Her robe was pulled aside completely and he pressed against her, making no secret of his desire.

All thoughts of resistance fled, as, moaning ecstatically, she abandoned herself to the insistent demand of his hands, as an intolerable aching pervaded her.

'Oh God, these last few weeks!' Tor said huskily. 'If you only knew what hell it's been, knowing that you were mine, unable to make love to you as fully as I wanted to, because you didn't remember me. How is it possible?' he asked wonderingly, his body thrusting fiercely against hers. 'To forget what we had, what we were to each other?'

'I don't know,' she whispered, 'I don't know.'
Her arms clasped tightly across his broad back,
her whole body seemed to throb as his caresses
extended their field of exploration.

'Say it then, Zara, say you still want me . . .
that you never wanted anyone else, that you want
to make love, the way we used to . . .'

Sudden revulsion swept through her, her mind
suddenly clear of the hypnotic effect of his
nearness. She stiffened in rejection. How could
she have allowed him to overcome her resolution?
There was no way they could go back. The past
was finished with, destroyed by Tor himself.

'Let go of me.' She tried to push him away.
'You're wrong, I don't want you.'

'No?' His tone was incredulous, but the gleam
of self-assurance was still in his eyes. 'That
wasn't the impression I was receiving.'

'I'm tired,' she snapped, 'weak. You took
advantage of that.'

His grasp of her had slackened and she turned
away from him, praying silently that she had said
sufficient to deter him. If he pressurised her she
knew she hadn't the strength, moral or physical,
to rebuff him again. There was a long, tense
silence.

'Look,' he said, after seemingly endless time
had elapsed, time in which Zara feared she might
move, without willing it, back into his embrace,
so violently did she long for him. 'We have a lot
of ground to cover, lost time to make up for . . .
explanations. But we have all our lives ahead of
us. I'm going to make a hot drink and then we're
going to discuss the future, rationally if we can
. . . and if we can't . . .' He made a gesture which

expressed all kinds of nuances, but above all, that the satisfaction of a mutual desire would render discussion needless. 'I can't believe that you've changed towards me so radically.'

She parted her lips to protest, turned towards him to tell him that, as she saw it, their problems were insoluble, the rift between their past and present lives too wide, that she still wouldn't consent to be his mistress even were she free. But he had gone and soon, distantly, she could hear the clink of cup against saucer.

Conscious of an all-enveloping weariness that encompassed spirit as well as body, she relaxed against the pillows, able to do so now that Tor's disturbing masculinity was removed from her orbit. She intended to think the situation through, then formulate reasoned, logical arguments that would persuade him of her future intentions, which were to leave Devon and to put the events of the last months firmly behind her, for ever. But somehow she never got beyond the first sentence and, heavy-eyed, drifted into the slumber of total mental and physical exhaustion.

CHAPTER EIGHT

TOR was very considerate. He didn't arouse her from the deep sleep into which she had fallen, but it only postponed the confrontation he had planned, and Zara woke next morning at first light, to find him stretched out close beside her, his intent gaze the first thing her own eyes met, as consciousness returned. Instantly, she experienced a dangerous, thrilling trembling, a hungry yearning, so that she wished desperately that she might open her arms to him, hold and be held. She sought for rational words to break the intensity of the moment, but Tor spoke first.

'Strange how it's all worked out,' he observed lazily, reaching out a caressing hand, with which to brush back the tangled hair from her sleep-flushed face. 'We've come full circle, haven't we? You're back in my bed, where you belong.'

Incensed by this immediate, provocative offensive, before she had scarcely had time to collect her wits, Zara sat up and only his restraining hand on her arm prevented her from sliding off the bed and leaving his room.

'I *don't* belong here,' she denied vehemently, 'and I intend to leave this place immediately, today. I'm going back to London.' There was none of the careful reasoning she had intended to use, the gradual working up to this statement.

'Don't be such a little fool, you don't mean that.' He tried to pull her down again and she had

to reject an impulse to surrender. 'Just as things
are working out for us at last. Now that you know
who you are, who I am. Oh, Zara!' he said, his
tone husky with remembered pain. 'When I stood
outside that church and watched you come out,
on Dane's arm, I thought that was the end of
everything. I . . .'

'So it *was* you,' she said, momentarily diverted.
'I thought so, but I couldn't be sure. You moved
away so quickly.'

'Because I couldn't stand the sight any longer.
But I didn't get far. Something kept me hovering
on the edge of the crowd, and I'm glad it did. I
saw them arrest Dane, heard enough to understand what was going on. I felt . . . I felt *exultant*.
I knew then that it wasn't all over, that I stood a
chance of getting you back.' His eyes swept
hungrily over her face, the curves of her body,
still concealed by the clinging material of his
robe.

'You never stood a chance of that,' she
contradicted, 'you still don't.'

'Oh I know that, technically, you're still
married to Dane, that it will take time, but . . .'

'Even if I do divorce him, it won't make any
difference,' she said flatly. 'I want to cut the past
right out of my life, to concentrate on my career.'
But only, her heart cried, because I don't mean to
you what you mean to me.

'You can still have a career, with *me*. I won't
object to your taking on other commissions, as
well as illustrating my books.'

Illustrating his books! That was what he
wanted her for! No mention still of love, or
marriage. Perhaps he thought she'd be more

complacent now about another kind of relationship ... since her disastrous association with
the Dane twins, married to one and ostensibly
living with the other as his wife. Maybe he still
thought she and Maurice ... Well, if he did, she
had to admit in all fairness, it was her own fault.
She had deliberately led him to believe ... But
that had been before her memory returned,
before she'd realised she didn't owe any loyalty to
Maurice Dane.

How oddly her life had been confused by the
existence of the twins. Even Nan Jones, with all
her wisdom, hadn't recognised the meaning of
what she had seen. 'Two men, so alike they have
you mazed between them.'

'I was in court too,' Tor said, breaking in upon
her unhappy reverie. 'The day Dane was sent
down. That was when I decided to write to you,
using my second name as an alias. I wanted to
help you, to erase that strained, unhappy look
from your face, wanted us to be together again.'

What far-reaching effects that letter had had,
Zara mused. Without it, Maurice might still have
perfected his plans for his twin's escape. His task
might have been that much more difficult, but it
might have succeeded without Tor's intervention.
And but for Tor's letter, there might have been
no need for her to have been dragged into it, no
need for her accident, for her loss of memory.
But the opportunity that letter presented had
been too good for Maurice to miss. So in a way it
was Tor's fault, everything that had happened to
her since. She told him so.

'It's all turned out for the best,' he said
unconcernedly.

'Well I don't agree. I feel ... feel such a fool, so embarrassed, to think of how I lived under your roof, for weeks, not knowing who you were, that you knew everything about me ... *everything*,' she repeated tremulously.

'And wearing your own clothes to boot.' Tor added to her fury, not bothering to conceal his amusement. 'But it really threw me,' he continued, suddenly grave, 'when you arrived here as *Maurice*'s wife, but only for a while. I'd already worked out what *he* was up to and then events pointed to Sybil as being his wife. Very convenient for him, your loss of memory. I take it that, until then, you *had* refused to co-operate in their plans?'

'Of course I had!'

'Well, it's all past history now.' The casual, matter-of-fact voice he had used for their discussion vanished, his tone becoming throaty. 'Now we can . . .'

'It's not *all* past,' she denied, swallowing nervously at the expression in his eyes. 'There's still . . .'

'Forget it, Zara, forget all of it,' he said, his voice husky, 'except the part that relates to us. Have you forgotten those times, when you were in my arms, when we nearly . . . the woods, the thunderstorm . . .?'

No she hadn't forgotten, she had so many other memories besides, and her breathing was as troubled as his, though she sought to conceal the fact.

'We've been given another chance, Zara. Don't let's waste it.' No longer tolerant of her withdrawal from him, he reached out a long arm and tugged her down, dragging her across the hairy roughness of his chest wall, his lips attempting to prise hers apart, to overcome her determined resistance. He held her tightly against him, letting her feel his need, his arms a strong, secure haven.

'Tor . . .'

'No,' he said masterfully, 'I gave in to you last night, because you were tired, suffering from shock, but this morning things are different . . .'

'They're not,' she said weakly but, in spite of herself, the moment he had touched her she knew she was lost, as aching desire sprang to life. It had never taken him long before, she remembered, to arouse her response to him.

It was as though, these past weeks, not only her brain, but her body too had been numb, anaesthetised by shock, and this sudden, almost violent return of sensation was as agonising as pins and needles to a cramped limb. His caresses were becoming kneadingly intimate and she could not remain cold towards him. Instead, her lips became soft, pliant, as his firm, assured kisses sparked off the desire that she knew was mutual. Her hands clasped about the strong muscles of his neck, her fingers plunging into the thick hair at his nape.

Her moans became feverish as she arched against him, murmuring his name over and over again in an ecstasy of longing. The feel of his body against hers was right, as though, until now, a part of her had been missing. His skin beneath her hands was warm, perspiration-dampened, exciting her, and she extended her explorations of his body, hearing his whispered 'yes, yes', through a haze of pleasurable sensation. Everything, even the past, had ceased to exist for her, nothing mattered except the way he was making her feel, the way *he* felt.

She moved sensuously against him and her pulses raced as he covered her, his body shuddering, his mouth fierce with his intense need, to which there could be only one outcome satisfactory to them both.

But it wasn't to be. Even as her thighs parted to embrace him, there came a thunderous knocking, which reverberated about the silent farmhouse, and for one wild moment, Zara thought it must be the pounding of their hearts.

It had been an omen, she decided later, a sign that their consummation was not to be, and as Tor, after a moment's angry rigidity, with an oath which expressed his frustration, pulled on slacks and sweater and went to investigate the disturbance, she made for the bathroom and a cold shower with which to restore her common sense.

As the shower cooled her body, her mind was able to shift to other considerations and it occurred to her to wonder who could be hammering on the farmhouse door at such an early hour. Her heart leapt in sudden alarm. It couldn't be Michael, could it? And Tor, made unwary by the mists of passion, had gone to open the door.

Heart pounding with fear, she ran to the other bedroom, to the wardrobe containing clothes which she now knew to be hers, scrambled her still damp body into fresh jeans and sweater.

Downstairs, on the threshold of the kitchen,

she paused to take in a great gulping breath of relief, for the man confronting Tor was no escaped convict, but a reassuringly large and solid policeman. He turned to face her.

'Ah, morning! Mrs Dane isn't it? Glad to see you were unharmed yesterday. I thought you and Mr Endacott should be brought up to date with events.'

She sat down on one of the hard kitchen chairs, eyes wide with remembrance of yesterday's panic.

'Have you . . . have you caught him?'

'No, not yet. But he can't have got far. We have road blocks and patrols out everywhere. May I suggest . . .' He paused. 'I don't want to alarm you, but I think it would be as well if you left the area for the duration, just until we can assure you of your safety.'

Though the need that prompted this suggestion sent waves of sickening fear through her, Zara saw in it the excuse she needed to leave the farm, to leave Tor, to escape from the havoc of her emotions. But what about Tor himself, if Michael returned?

'If it would be any help, Ma'am,' the officer continued, 'I'll be passing the railway station on my way in to make my report.'

Tor intervened, his tone curt.

'I intend going up to London myself, as soon as I've arranged for someone to come in and look after the animals.'

'I'd rather go now,' Zara said hastily. 'I don't want to spend a moment longer in this place.'

'I think you're very wise,' the officer commented. He couldn't know that, at the thought of remaining, she was beset by fears unconnected with her husband. If Tor were to renew his attempts to persuade her, she wasn't sure she could resist him, in fact she was sure she couldn't and there might not be another fortuitous interruption.

'I'll go and pack,' she said and turned swiftly on her heel, leaving the kitchen before Tor could protest further. He could scarcely make a scene in front of the policeman, she reasoned, having no legal right to keep her here. But if she allowed the police car to leave without her, she knew there would be a disturbing confrontation, in which both anger and other more insidious wiles would be brought to bear.

Even so, Zara thought, looking back just a week later, Tor had shown his displeasure very clearly, and if she hadn't known better, she would have thought his eyes also betrayed hurt at her determined defection. But she had known better and she wouldn't stay to be used by a man who didn't love her in every sense of the word, mere physical attraction wasn't enough.

It had been a wrench, though, to leave the farmhouse, unable to bid Tor a proper farewell, to know that she was at last leaving for ever, and she was glad the police officer was kept busy receiving and transmitting messages, so that little was required of her in the way of conversation.

'Where the deuce have you been hiding yourself for the past few weeks?' Zara's agent enquired indignantly, when he walked into her new flat.

'Oh . . . in the country,' she replied evasively. 'Sorry I couldn't let you know before.' She felt she couldn't bear to relate, just yet, her experiences of the past weeks, even to a friend of such long standing.

She'd telephoned to advise Charlie Laing of her new address, for, immediately on her return to London, she'd given up her former flat, in an attempt to cover her tracks, not only from Michael Dane, should he be so foolish as to seek her out in London, but also from Tor.

'I've half a dozen jobs lined up for you here,' Charlie continued, his wrath unappeased. 'This is no time to be taking country breaks. Besides, I thought you'd become a workaholic since that dreadful affair of your marriage. When can you come round to the office and . . .?'

'That's what I wanted to see you about,' Zara interrupted. 'I don't *want* to come into the office, Charlie, not just at the moment. There's . . . there's someone I don't want to risk meeting. Could . . . could you come to me for a time, and keep my whereabouts strictly confidential?'

'Has this anything to do with Tor Endacott, by any chance?'

'Yes, since you ask,' Zara said defiantly, 'it has.'

'Hmmm. I wondered why he'd been haunting the place this last week.'

Zara drew in a deep, unsteady breath. She wasn't really surprised that Tor had tried to find her. She'd already known he wouldn't give up so easily. In one sense she was glad, but it was disturbing too, this evidence of his persistence. She couldn't spend her life avoiding him.

With Charlie's reluctant agreement that he wouldn't reveal her new address to anyone and that henceforth, for the time being at least, *he* would call upon *her* to discuss commissions, Zara felt more able to relax, but not entirely. She might have put a few hundred miles between herself and Wolfstor Farm, the recollections it held for her, but Tor couldn't be kept at such a distance and she couldn't banish memory.

Then too, there was the ever-present fear that somehow Michael Dane might catch up with her, though she hoped he'd managed to leave the country.

So Tor was in London, now, pestering Charlie for news of her. Would Charlie be able to stand firm, not swayed by the fact that Tor too was a valued friend and client? In fact Charlie was now her only link with the man she still loved. When he brought round the promised work, even though it would be more sensible to avoid the subject, she knew she would question him as to Tor's well-being, the only way she could obtain news of him, something, she was forced to admit, that was still necessary to her, would perhaps always be a necessity. Would his absence from her life ever cease to hurt?

But before Charlie's next visit, Zara received another, unexpected one. Convinced that Michael had by now managed to make good his escape, she hadn't expected to hear anything further from the police and when she saw the two uniformed figures at her door, she assumed they were there to confirm their failure to retake their prisoner.

The two officers, one male, one female, followed her into her sitting-room, where she stood, hands clasped anxiously in the folds of her skirt. If only this weren't necessary. If only she could be allowed to forget Michael's existence altogether and her own unhappy involvement with him.

'Please sit down, Mrs Dane,' the female officer suggested. 'What we have to say may come as a shock.'

Wonderingly, she obeyed, looking from one to the other. What could they have to tell her that was worse than anything that had already happened?

'When you escaped from your husband's getaway car that night, had you any idea of your precise location?'

'No, it was foggy. I was afraid . . . scared stiff. I'd lost all sense of direction.'

'Then it would surprise you to know that you were within only fifty yards or so of the Wolfstor Mire?'

Zara shuddered. It did surprise her, horrified her. Suppose her frenzied, stumbling escape had taken her into the mire, instead of in the opposite direction? But why had they seen fit to tell her this, adding another dimension to her nightmare recollections?

'When our patrols failed to pick up your husband—and we were pretty sure he couldn't have evaded them—we had to consider other possibilities. Mrs Dane, there's no way we can soften this news. I'm afraid your husband is dead. His body was recovered yesterday, from the Wolfstor Mire.'

Zara sat still, totally speechless, violent emotions warring within her. There was shock, there was overwhelming relief, but there was pity too, for Michael, for his wasted life. After all, she had been fond of him . . . once. She pulled herself together with a conscious effort. Some response was required of her.

'Thank you for telling me,' she said quietly, too quietly, so that they looked at her with some concern.

'Is there anyone you'd like us to send for, to be with you?' the woman asked gently.

Zara shook her head. There was only one person she longed to turn to, to cling to, but pride forbade she should ever seek help from Tor.

'There's no one. But don't worry, I'll be quite all right, when I get used to the idea.'

Reluctantly, they agreed to leave her alone, and Zara could hardly wait to close the door behind them. But now she must face this new situation, and despite the fact that now she was free, waves of horror, the waste of it all, swept over her. She wondered if Tor would get to hear of Michael's death and supposed that much was inevitable. Even if he didn't receive a personal communication, the story was bound to be featured by the news media. How would it affect him? Undoubtedly he'd be glad for her sake, but ... The doorbell's summons interrupted this line of thought, and for a moment or two, she was tempted to ignore it. But it might be the police again, and if she didn't answer, they might fear the worst and break in.

'Charlie! It's you! Come in!'

Her agent carried two bulging folders as well as his briefcase, and he heaved a great sigh of relief as she opened the door.

'Thank goodness you're in. I wouldn't want to cart this lot back to the office. I lost your number and with you being ex-directory now ...' As he dumped his paperwork and sank on to the settee, he realised something was amiss. 'You look a bit fraught, my girl. What's up?'

About to allow herself the luxury of pouring out her recent troubles, she was distracted yet again by the necessity of answering the door. It didn't even occur to her to wonder who it could be this time, even though only Charlie and the police had her current address, and she was taken entirely by surprise, as control of the door was taken from her nerveless hand. As though he expected her to resist him, Tor was across the threshold in one swift, powerful move and a disconcerted Zara found herself trailing meekly after him. How had he discovered her whereabouts?

'Charlie?' she began accusingly. 'I thought I told you . . .'

'Don't blame Charlie,' Tor interrupted brusquely. 'He doesn't know it, but I've followed him everywhere he's been for the past two or three days. I knew he'd have to contact you sooner or later.' He turned to their mutual agent. 'Do me a favour, old chap. Get lost. Come back another day, hmmm?'

After one comprehensive glance from Zara, to Tor and back again, Charlie complied, though not without protest.

'When am I going to get some work out of this girl? There are manuscripts waiting to go into print, only needing the illustrations.'

'You can have all the work out of her you like,' Tor told him, 'in about a month's time. No, don't argue. You'll only be wasting your time . . . and mine.' He hustled the older man out of the flat.

Zara discovered that her legs were suddenly incapable of holding her and she sank into the seat vacated by Charlie, waiting with fearful, quivering expectancy for Tor's return. He didn't keep her waiting long and as the door slammed behind the agent, two or three strides brought him back to stand over her, an expression in his eyes she found impossible to fathom.

'Wh . . . what do you want?' she whispered, when she could bear the tense silence no longer.

He gave a short crack of laughter, laughter that held no amusement.

'What I've always wanted . . . you.'

'Please,' she begged him, her composure already strained to the limit, 'don't start all that again. I . . . I don't think I can take any more.'

'Zara!' He seated himself beside her, totally overpowering at such close quarters, and possessed himself of one tremulous hand. 'We have to be realistic about this. O.K., so a lot of bad things have happened. We've had misunderstandings. But these can all be straightened out. You'll put in for a divorce, naturally, but I don't want to wait until then to take care of you. You must let me . . .'

'There won't be any need for a divorce,' she said dully. Obviously, he hadn't heard. The news was always released to the next of kin before it was made public.

'What do you mean?' His tone was one of outrage. 'You can't mean you intend to stay tied to that . . . that . . .'

'Tor, please,' her voice quivered, 'whatever he was, whatever he's done, you mustn't . . . you mustn't speak ill of the dead.'

It was his turn to be stunned into silence, but it was a silence which didn't last long.

'*Dead?* Dane? You mean . . .? You've had news? When?' The questions seemed to ricochet about her downbent head.

She nodded and for the first time since she'd heard of Michael's death, felt her lips quiver betrayingly. It was Tor's nearness that was doing it, weakening her resolve to be strong.

'This morning . . . about half an hour ago,' she managed to say, before her control lapsed completely and she dragged her fingers from his clasp, both hands covering her face as she dissolved into sobs that racked her whole frame.

His arms went about her, a steel-strong circle, and she was where she had longed to be, ever since she had heard of the violent nature of her release from her marriage. It couldn't be wrong to seek a little comfort, she thought incoherently, just for a few moments.

But it was nearly twenty minutes later, before she had sobbed out all the misery that seemed to have accumulated for so long, perhaps since her first parting with Tor, before her foolish, ill-considered marriage.

She wasn't certain when his comforting embrace began to express other emotions, but as she quieted, he drew her closer and lifted her face to his, to begin a very thorough and comprehensive quest with his lips, over cheeks, damp eyelids and still quivering mouth. Drained by the storm of feeling that had swept her, she was powerless to resist, knew she didn't really *want* to resist. His hands were on the pointed fullness of her breasts, the warmth of his touch sensuously arousing.

'You're not grieving for Dane?' he asked her suddenly.

'Not in the way you mean,' she whispered. 'It
is awful though, to think of someone you've
known . . . such a horrible way to die too. But,'
her voice trembled, 'I feel guilty, because I'm so
relieved, that I'm free of him. Is it . . . is it
wicked of me to think that way?'

'Not at all,' he said positively. 'You owe him
no loyalty. As to the manner of his death, I don't
think Dane would have taken kindly to the idea of
being cooped up for life. But enough of him,
Zara. Without wishing to sound callous, we *have*
to forget him, to think of ourselves.' His hands
moved down to encompass the bones of her hips,
caressingly, proprietorially.

'Ourselves?' She shook her head. There was
no way their futures could be linked together.

'Zara, listen to me,' he commanded, as
he continued to shape her body with his hands,
unhurriedly,   seductively.   'We've   wasted
enough time in separations, misunderstandings.
We've been given another chance. Let's take
it.'

He proceeded to demonstrate just how *he*
intended to utilise *his* opportunities, in a very
positive fashion, with lips, with hands, with all
the hard, taut muscles of his body held against
her, all allies in the onslaught that was all but
demolishing her defences. As his mouth quelled
all possibility of protest on her part, as his fingers
sought, found, caressed, possessed, sought to
arouse, she felt her stomach tighten, the fierce,
warm throb of sensation one akin to pain in the
very depths of her. He was kissing her, using
every facet of his sensual expertise, preventing
her from drawing away from him, as the pressure

of his body grew in intensity.

At first she was determinedly rigid, trying to convince herself that she was frozen to all feelings, incapable of response. But he was a master of the art he practised and slowly but surely he awakened physical pleasure in her, pleasure that would soon become an urgent need, so that she ached with the effort of combating the awakening. A sexual stimulus on its own had no connection with love as she perceived it.

'Tor,' breathlessly she managed to evade his possessive lips, 'you can't just walk in here and . . .'

'And take up where we left off? Why not?' Undeterred, his hands were moving towards ever more intimate possession, evoking sharp, sweet sensuality, and Zara felt as though she were melting, floating, head swimming, making coherent thought impossible.

'I *want* you, Zara!' The words rang insistently through her bemused brain. 'I want you, now. We've waited long enough.'

'No, I . . .' She moved her head from side to side, trying to escape the enslavement his lips forced upon her, trying to deny this enticing madness of the flesh.

'You want me too. You always have, no use denying it. Why are you trying to deny it, Zara?'

Determination to have this out with him once and for all gave her the strength to thrust him away.

'Because I won't do what you want me to do, be your mistress. It's true I've made a pretty ghastly mess of my life up to now. But even if I did choose the wrong man, at least we were married and I'm not going to make another mistake. I'm not going to compromise with what I believe to be right.' She glared at him defiantly.

His face expressed astonishment and of his own volition he moved further away from her.

'Let me get this straight. You think I'm only interested in having an affair with you?'

'Yes.' Somehow she managed to maintain the defiance. 'I *know* that's all you want. You made that quite clear.'

'Oh my God!' He ran his hands through his hair creating wild disorder. 'Damn it, Zara, I want to *marry* you. I admit that when we first met I would have settled for your love on any terms. You seemed totally dedicated to your career, as eager as me to be free of any commitments. I admit it shook me, when I realised you expected marriage, and at first I just wasn't prepared to give up my freedom. I even spent several weeks telling myself I *could* do without you, that if I didn't see you, I'd get over whatever ailed me. But then I realised I was a hopeless case, incurable, that I was in love, a state I'd never imagined. I came back, intending to tell you so, to ask you if you'd forgive me for my insensitiveness, to ask you to marry me. But the very day I came back, you married Dane.'

'I . . . I thought you only wanted me, because you wanted a tame illustrator for your books.' She faltered at the look in his eyes, almost black with fury.

'You have a very strange conception of my character. I'm not so calculating. Misguided, mistaken maybe, but never that.' Restlessly, he moved away from her, and paced about the room, his words coming angrily, jerkily. 'Haven't you realised yet, even after all we've gone through together in the past weeks? Did you really think I was only indulging in an experiment? I wanted to help you, yes, hoped it would restore your memory, but I also saw your amnesia as an opportunity to make you fall in love with me again. You couldn't remember your real husband, and I was pretty sure you weren't in love with him anyway. I had more faith than you. I didn't believe you could fall in and out of love so quickly! And if you *had* been fond of him, what he'd done would surely have opened your eyes. When your memory came back, I wanted to be there, to pick up the pieces, to offer you the love and security I knew you'd need, that I wanted to give you . . . belatedly, admittedly.'

'You . . . you never mentioned love,' she pointed out, not daring to let the tiny seed of hope he had planted grow to fruition.

'Didn't I? I said I wanted you and that was true. I did want you, but I thought you realised that need implied *everything*. I wanted you . . . *want* you in every way, Zara.' His voice thickened and he returned to her, took her, unresisting, into his arms. 'I want to share everything with you, for the rest of my life, and I don't mean just the ecstasy of our bodies in close union. I want us to share experiences of every kind, all that's in our minds, our hearts, souls, if you believe in such things.'

It was hard to realise that the veil was finally lifted, to realise that this was not only her lover, but her love, had always been so. She wound her arms about his waist, felt him tremble, knew he waited in trepidation for her answer.

'I believe in everything that you believe in,' she

murmured softly, standing on tiptoe, her lips against his throat, where a pulse leapt agitatedly. 'And that's the kind of sharing I want too.'

'And love?' he asked. 'You do love me?'

'Yes, I love you,' she told him joyfully. 'I've always loved you, but I thought . . .'

He didn't wait to hear her repeat all their misunderstandings, but with a great cry of exultation, swung her up into his arms.

'I told Charlie no work for a month,' he whispered throatily against her hair. 'Make that two months.'

It didn't take him long to free them of their clothing, for she was his willing assistant, sharing his urgency. Even so, he did not rush this precious moment, but with leisurely mastery stirred her body, with unerring sureness of purpose, allowing her too her moments of exploration of muscled contours that hardened and quickened beneath her discovering hands. Then he drew her closer and she felt the warmth, the seductive suppleness of his naked body against her own, its needs of her urgently apparent.

'Oh my darling, oh, Tor, love me,' she cried. 'Love me, please.'

'Every day, every moment of our lives,' he confirmed, his thigh imprisoning hers, the pressure intensifying, igniting passion.

For a few exquisite moments, she hovered between agony and ecstasy and then they confirmed their commitment to each other, by sharing that greatest gift vouchsafed to them, a gift that time and usage could not weary or make commonplace.

AT LAST YOU CAN FIND
TRUE ROMANCE ON TELEVISION!

PRESENTING THE SHOWTIME●

S E R I E S

Full-scale romance movies, taken from your favorite Harlequin novels. Beautifully photographed on location, it's romance the way you've always dreamed. Exclusively on Showtime cable TV!

HARLEQUIN ON SHOWTIME
COMING ATTRACTIONS:

LOVE WITH A PERFECT STRANGER. Based on the Pamela Wallace novel, starring MARILU HENNER.

ONLY ON SHOWTIME

EXCLUSIVE MOVIES ("Beverly Hills Cop," "Witness")–EXCLUSIVE AWARD-WINNING SERIES ("Brothers," "Faerie Tale Theatre," "The Paper Chase") –EXCLUSIVE COMEDY SPECIALS ("Jay Leno," "Don Rickles")–EXCLUSIVE MUSIC EVENTS ("Aretha Franklin," "Motown On Showtime") and now. . .

HARLEQUIN ON SHOWTIME – THE ONLY
PLACE ON TV TO FIND TRUE ROMANCE!

CALL YOUR CABLE COMPANY TODAY TO ORDER SHOWTIME
(U.S. ONLY)
ST-H

Take 4 novels and a surprise gift FREE

Here's how to get this special offer from Harlequin!

November
BETTY NEELS
TREASURY EDITION
COUPON

As simple as 1...2...3!

1. **Each month, save one Treasury Edition coupon from your favorite Romance or Presents novel.**
2. **In four months you'll have saved four Treasury Edition coupons (only one coupon per month allowed).**
3. **Then all you have to do is fill out and return the order form provided, along with the four Treasury Edition coupons required and $2.95 for postage and handling.**

Mail to: Harlequin Reader Service

In the U.S.A.
901 Fuhrmann Blvd.
P.O. Box 1397
Buffalo, NY 14240

In Canada
P.O. Box 609
Fort Erie, Ontario
L2A 9Z9

BN-Nov-2

Please send me my Special copy of the Betty Neels Treasury Edition. I have enclosed the four Treasury Edition coupons required and $2.95 for postage and handling along with this order form. (Please Print)

NAME_____

ADDRESS_____

CITY_____

STATE/PROV._____ ZIP/POSTAL CODE_____

SIGNATURE_____

This offer is limited to one order per household.

This special Betty Neels offer expires
February 28, 1987.

SUPPLIES LIMITED

Janet Dailey
Americana

Don't miss a single title from this great collection. The first eight titles have already been published. Complete and mail this coupon today to order books you may have missed.

Harlequin Reader Service
In U.S.A.
901 Fuhrmann Blvd.
P.O. Box 1397
Buffalo, N.Y. 14140

In Canada
P.O. Box 2800
Postal Station A
5170 Yonge Street
Willowdale, Ont. M2N 6J3

Please send me the following titles from the Janet Dailey Americana Collection. I am enclosing a check or money order for $2.75 for each book ordered, plus 75¢ for postage and handling.

_____	ALABAMA	Dangerous Masquerade
_____	ALASKA	Northern Magic
_____	ARIZONA	Sonora Sundown
_____	ARKANSAS	Valley of the Vapours
_____	CALIFORNIA	Fire and Ice
_____	COLORADO	After the Storm
_____	CONNECTICUT	Difficult Decision
_____	DELAWARE	The Matchmakers

Number of titles checked @ $2.75 each = $_____

N.Y. RESIDENTS ADD
   APPROPRIATE SALES TAX $_____

Postage and Handling $___.75___

                    TOTAL $_____

I enclose _____

(Please send check or money order. We cannot be responsible for cash sent through the mail.)

PLEASE PRINT

NAME _____

ADDRESS _____

CITY _____

STATE/PROV. _____

BLJD-A-1